# COASTAL JURY

## COASTAL ADVENTURE SERIES 9

### DON RICH

Copyright © 2022 by Florida Refugee Press LLC

All rights reserved.

No portion of this book may be reproduced in any form without written permission from the publisher or author,

COASTAL JURY by Don Rich.

No part of this book may be reproduced, scanned, or distributed in any printed or electronic form without written permission or as permitted by U.S. copyright law. Please do not participate in or encourage piracy of copyrighted materials in violation of the author's rights. Purchase only authorized editions.

Library of Congress PCN Data

Rich, Don

Coastal Jury/Don Rich

Florida Refugee Press LLC

Cover by: Cover2Book.com

This is a work of fiction. Names, characters, and incidents are either the product of the author's imagination or are used fictitiously. Any resemblance to actual persons, living or dead, businesses, companies, events, or locales is purely coincidental. However, the overall familiarity with boats and water found in this book comes from the author having spent years on, under, and beside them.

Published by FLORIDA REFUGEE PRESS, LLC, 2022

Crozet, VA

# CONTENTS

| | |
|---|---|
| Prologue | 1 |
| 1. A Fresh Start | 5 |
| 2. Overdue Interest | 13 |
| 3. Honest Front | 25 |
| 4. Changes | 30 |
| 5. Sand Dancers | 38 |
| 6. The Summons | 46 |
| 7. New Friends | 54 |
| 8. Inside Scoop | 62 |
| 9. One Badass | 70 |
| 10. Wave Dancer | 82 |
| 11. The Offer | 92 |
| 12. A Visitor | 100 |
| 13. Redecorating | 108 |
| 14. Complications | 114 |
| 15. A Plan & A First | 125 |
| 16. Goodbyes | 133 |
| 17. Worse Things | 142 |
| 18. Paybacks | 151 |
| 19. Heavy Price To Pay | 159 |
| 20. Rut's Fight | 168 |
| 21. Coincidences | 178 |
| Epilogue | 185 |
| Glossary | 192 |
| *About the Author* | 199 |
| *Also by Don Rich* | 201 |

*To my pal and fellow TropicalAuthors.com member, Nicholas Harvey, aka: "BritNick." Thanks for the encouragement, guidance, the friendship as well as for "giving your all" in Coastal Curse, LOL!*

# PROLOGUE

Sean "Rut" Rutledge set the GPS down next to the other units on his desktop then leaned back in his chair, his eyelids closing to a squint. The barely twenty-year-old idiot on the other side of his desk didn't seem to notice that Rut was getting mad, or worse, he didn't care if he did. He kept rambling on about how easy it had been to steal the electronics and get away without being spotted. Finally, Rut held up his hand, interrupting him.

"Do you have any idea what you've done? Who you've stolen from?"

At first the kid looked startled, then confused. "Naw, they wasn't around. Like I was tellin' you, I got away clean."

"You're a damned 'come here' moron."

"What the hell's a 'come here?'"

Rut sighed. The kid was more interested in finding out about the "come here" part than he was insulted by being called a moron. "It's somebody who wasn't born here on the Eastern Shore. Which partly explains why you were dumb enough to steal from a local waterman. And before you ask, a waterman is somebody who makes a living by fishing, crabbing, or oystering. It's hard work, done by even harder people. Did you happen to see the name scratched into the back of that GPS? It's Andy Albury. You better thank your lucky stars he didn't catch you, because nobody would've ever found your body if he had."

Now the kid looked insulted. "Freddy Vaca said you're the one to deal with to get rid of some stuff. An' I got this stuff. But you ain't no fence, you're some kinda poser."

Rut said, "No, I'm not a fence." He picked up his phone and snapped the kid's picture.

"Hey! What the hell's that for!"

"That," Rut said, "is for Andy, so he'll know who to look for. And if I were you, I'd get the heck off the Eastern Shore and over to the mainland as fast as I could go, then I'd make it a point never to come back over here if you want to keep breathing."

The kid glared at him and reached for the first of the electronics.

Rut said, "Leave it."

"Like hell! It's mine, and I'm taking it with me." He pulled a switchblade from his pocket, brandishing it at Rut from across the desk as he continued to reach for that nearest unit. He froze in mid-reach as Rut's other hand came out from under his desk. In it was a stainless-steel revolver with a long barrel and a huge bore. Rut aimed at the center of the kid's torso, and the look in his eye said he was as serious as a heart attack.

"I said leave it. And drop that knife while you're at it." He saw the kid glance sideways at the open doorway and he added, "You'll never make it."

The kid threw the knife at Rut, hoping to distract him while he made for the door. It went way wide, missing Rut entirely. Rut let him clear the door before taking a shot, aiming past the travel lift piers and out into Mockhorn Bay beyond. The sound of the Model 629 Smith & Wesson .44 magnum was deafening inside Rut's small office. He was removing the spent shell from the cylinder wheel when Big Jim Jordan burst into the office. The massive black man was carrying a three-foot length of pipe up at an angle like it was his turn at bat. He gave the room a quick scan as he entered.

"Rut, you all right?"

"No! Every time I shoot this damn thing without ear protection, my ears ring for a week."

"You missed him!"

"I meant to. If I'd have wanted to hit him, there'd be bits and pieces of him all over the place, and then I'd have to repaint the place. But I bet he has to change his drawers."

"Hell, I may have to change mine! He's lucky you can't shoot straight. What'd he do to get shot at anyway?"

"Again, if I had wanted to hit... oh, never mind." He motioned to the stuff on his desk. "He robbed Andy Albury's boat."

"Holy... he's lucky it was you with the gun and not Andy."

"You know, I still have five bullets left." He slid a new round into the revolver's empty chamber. "Now six."

Big Jim laughed. "Five or six, it don't matter. I still like my chances since you're the one holdin' the gun."

Rut returned the pistol to the hidden holster attached under the desk as he glared at Jim. "Okay, smart guy, how about getting ahold of Freddy Vaca and telling him he needs to be more careful about what he says to people if he ever wants any favors from me again. He told the kid I was a fence. I should never have sold Freddy anything, but I felt bad for him after his boat sunk so I cut him a real deal on some 'gently used' electronics. That'll teach me to try and help people. I'll call Andy and let him know we've got his stuff and a picture of the 'come here' who took it. If the kid has any sense at all, he'll be back over the bridge before Andy gets here." The bridge he referred to was the Chesapeake Bay Bridge-Tunnel, a seventeen-and-a-half-mile long structure that stretches across the mouth of the Chesapeake Bay. It connects the Virginia Beach area with the tip of the Eastern Shore of Virginia peninsula, commonly known as ESVA. "And Vaca needs to know I don't buy anything from anywhere around here, especially when it's taken from a waterman. I'm not going to take food out of their families' mouths."

"I'll take care of it. Vaca's just dumb. I can't fix dumb or teach him how to tell who he can or can't trust to keep quiet. But I can scare him into keeping his mouth shut instead." He took his pipe and went back out into the boatyard.

Rut took a tissue and picked up the kid's knife, being careful not to get any of his own fingerprints or DNA on it. You never know where the kid might have gotten it, or in what crimes it might have been used, and whose DNA might still be on it. Then he had an idea and walked out into the boatyard over to the twin piers of the travel lift's haul-out slip. Once he was out at the end of one of the piers, he glanced around to make sure there weren't any prying eyes, then he tossed the knife into the deep water of the slip where it would soon sink down into the muck. Not that anyone in his boatyard would've cared or said anything if they'd seen him do this, whether they were one of his employees or even a customer. His boatyard catered mostly to workboats, and their owners pretty much minded their own business. And Rut had a reputation for being a tough character, even though for the most part it was unearned. If anyone besides Big Jim heard the shot earlier it would just add to that image, and he didn't want to discourage it. You never know when it might keep someone from doing something dumb.

# 1

## A FRESH START

Rut was in his mid-forties, almost two inches under six feet tall, with a lean build and some gray starting to creep into his brown hair. The real truth about him was that he had for years been totally legitimate, making a meager but honest living with his Mockhorn Boat Works business. Then an unexpected divorce turned his world upside down. It had left him piled with debt, even though he and his ex had no children, and she had been the one who had cheated on him. She also had a better divorce attorney. Rut was squeezed almost to the breaking point, and had been forced to borrow money from Michael "Mango" Magnowski, a loan shark from Virginia Beach, in order to save his business and home. Rut had barely been able to make the interest payments, and he had no illusions about what would happen to him if he fell behind. Mango had several "leg-breakers" on his payroll.

Then a new customer showed up at the yard in an old thirty-six-foot *Hatteras* sportfisherman; a real scow. The boat was from Miami, and the owner turned out to be a likable guy. He and Rut had a few beers that first night, and over the course of the evening it came out that he had some "extra" fishing tackle to sell. It was all really high-end stuff, and what he was willing to take for it was a steal. A real steal. Because it had all been stolen down in South Florida. He said he knew where he could get his hands on a lot more of it when he got back down there, so he was willing to trade this batch for his yard bill. Most of the larger sportfishing boats carry enough tackle so that it's not uncommon for the combined cost to be well into the mid to high five-figures, retail. What the man was offering was enough to completely outfit any one of those boats.

Maybe it was the few beers Rut had already consumed by that point, or maybe it was his realizing this one deal could get him out of the hole where he'd found himself with Mango, or at the very least buy him some time. More likely it was a combination of all the above. In any case, he accepted the guy's offer. The next day it turned out that this deal bought him more than just time since Mango had recently bought a boat and had begun shopping for tackle. He was impressed with both the gear as well as the price Rut quoted him for it. Much higher than the Miami guy's yard bill, but still a fraction of retail. He wanted to know if Rut could find more like it. Another deal like this one would cancel out the rest of what Rut owed him.

Knowing his new friend had said he had access to a lot of similar deals, Rut countered that if Mango would front him the cash, he might be able to do another couple of deals like this if Mango could find an outlet for the goods. And so began a new business for Rut, one that paid in cash and was ultimately financed by the insurance industry in South Florida. Tackle and electronics theft were both rampant down there, and the biggest issue for the thieves was to find a place where they could unload the merchandise without getting caught. The cops were constantly watching the internet sites as well as the local pawn shops, and that was where many of the thieves got tripped up. But nobody thought to look for the stuff up in the mid-Atlantic.

That night over more beers with his new Miami friend, they came to an agreement on double the amount of tackle, with his friend handling the shipping. And so Rut was instantly lifted out of debt, while being launched into this shady yet very profitable business. But he wanted it understood by his Miami contact that he didn't want to know where any of it came from. In fact, he wanted phony receipts for it all to be included in the shipment. Not that it would be the best defense if he was ever caught, but at least it was something to work with. And Mango was supposedly "connected," so Rut at least had a little cover here on this end. He wasn't sure exactly who was on Mango's payroll, maybe some cops or even a judge or two, and frankly, he didn't want to know. He made it clear to everyone that he wasn't interested in becoming involved beyond facilitating the shipments of merchandise. Of course, that didn't mean he'd stay limited to supplying only Virginia Beach.

Soon Rut and Mango had added connections in Ocean City, Rehoboth Beach, Atlantic City, and several other cities throughout the mid-Atlantic. They quickly branched out into electronics as well. At first, Mango tried his best to find out who Rut's southern connection was so he could bypass him, but Rut was too savvy for that. He knew if it ever happened, that would be the end of the gravy train for him. And he knew if Mango ever needed a patsy, he'd be the one that got named. Rut was nothing if not careful. He made sure that they moved just enough of a steady flow of goods without being too greedy and ending up getting caught. Also, Rut wasn't stupid about where he spent his extra cash. Being a recycled bachelor, he mostly ate lunch and dinner out, sometimes with company. Plus, he also kept several large stacks of cash in a safe that was hidden in his home, just in case of emergencies. The rest of the cash he ran through his business. Work orders for boats that never existed were the perfect tools for laundering cash. Yes, it meant he had to pay tax on it, but then the "profit" could go right into his bank account without raising any suspicion. Big Jim helped with this side business, and was well paid in cash for his part as well as for his loyalty. Truthfully, Rut couldn't have handled it without him. Like Rut, Big Jim understood the importance of being careful about where he spent the extra cash. There would be a bit more of it this week in appreciation for Big Jim charging into Rut's office to check on him after hearing that shot. Friendship and loyalty were two things that Rut valued most, and so did Big Jim.

. . .

Rut called Andy Albury from out at the end of the travel lift's pier. From Andy's tone Rut could tell he was having a really bad day, which he'd already anticipated. Like so many of the local watermen's boats, Andy's hadn't been insured for its contents. He went from angry to ecstatic when he heard Rut's news, and said he'd be right over. Rut had no sooner hung up when his phone rang. Mango.

"Hey, Mango."

"Hey, you at your boatyard?"

"Yes?"

"Good. I'm about five minutes out. I needya ta haul my boat and clean the bottom. I got a tournament this weekend, and I wanna make sure I can get every ounce a speed outta her."

Rut knew it would have taken a good hour of running for Mango to reach his yard. "You have to have passed a half dozen places where you could've gotten hauled. Why are you running all the way up here?"

"Because all those other guys woulda charged me. I'll see you in five, partner." He hung up before Rut could say anything.

"Yeah, you're welcome," Rut replied to a silent phone. Footing Mango's yard bill hadn't been an agreed-upon part of their deal, but apparently now was going to be an added cost of doing business with him. He walked over to the travel lift, fired up the diesel engine, and then climbed aboard. Driving it out to where it straddled the twin piers, he lowered the heavy-duty nylon lifting slings down into the water. He'd just finished when Mango's boat came into view.

Big Jim had also walked out onto the pier when he recognized who was running the boat. He didn't like Mango, and knew Rut couldn't fully trust the guy. But he also understood why he needed him. "Don't tell me, lemme guess. It's a freebie."

Rut scowled and said, "Yeah. But we'll book it anyway. Double the time and change the boat name on the cash ticket. I don't want any paperwork that can connect him with us or the business. Oh, and

Andy's on his way over to pick up his stuff. If I'm busy with Mango, you mind handling that for me? I don't want Mango near him."

"Got it."

Mango pulled slowly into the slip and over the wide slings. Rut throttled up the travel lift engine and then raised the slings until he took up the slack, cradling the hull. When Mango killed his engines, Rut raised the boat until the bow's deck was level with the top of the seawall. He moved the boat closer to land, allowing Mango to simply step off the bow over onto the seawall. Then he continued raising the boat until the running gear cleared the top of the seawall so he could drive the lift off the piers and over to the pressure washing area where his crew would scrape and clean the bottom. Then climbing off the lift, he joined Mango as he inspected the hull.

"I gotta use this thing more. Lotsa crap growin' on her bottom."

Rut replied, "It would help. Did you say you are in a tournament this weekend?"

"Yeah, why?"

Rut crouched down and duckwalked over to the starboard shaft. He grabbed and shook it. There shouldn't have been any sideways movement, but it wiggled a bit. "Mango, didn't you notice a vibration or a noise?" When Mango shrugged, Rut continued. "Your cutlass bearing in the strut on this side is shot. The rubber is almost totally gone."

"What's a cutlass bearing?"

Rut sighed, and then pointed to the strut. "It's the rubber sleeve inside the strut that the shaft runs through. With this one totally worn out, it'll be making more noise underwater than a heavy metal concert, at least as far as the fish are concerned."

"What'll it cost you to fix it?"

Rut caught the inference, and wasn't going to let it slide. "I'll give the bearing to you at cost, and okay, I'll eat the labor. Probably take an hour or two after they get through washing the bottom."

Mango was irritated at being charged anything. "Well, then the least you can do is buy me lunch at the *Cove Beach Bar*. Sounds like we'll have plenty of time."

*Mallard Cove Marina* was a popular place with the boating community. Situated on the tip of the ESVA peninsula, among other amenities it had two beach bars that stayed busy all through the warmer months, and were favorites of Rut's. He paused before replying, but then figured it would be better to have Mango down there where there were more distractions, than to have him parked in the office with Rut as a captive audience.

"All right, let's go, but we'll flip to see who pays. It'll give the yard crew time to get all of that done while we're gone." He led Mango over toward his truck when he saw a familiar figure climbing over the seawall, having just moored a very ragged-looking Carolina Skiff with weird purple-colored bottom paint. The boat was filled with barrels and large homemade baitwells. It didn't appear to have been washed in years, if ever. Neither did the man.

"Hey, Daniels."

"Hey, Rut. Jes' makin' a supply run ta get some liquor an' some fuel in th' cans for mah backup gennie." The man was probably in his seventies, though it was hard to tell. He was about five feet, eight inches tall, with a slight build, scraggly gray hair and a beard to match that looked like it had bits of old food caught in it. His worn clothes had that "five days of fish slime buildup" on them. He headed for an old rusty sedan that was parked next to Rut's passenger door, where Mango was now standing. Daniels's car had been hand-painted with boat enamel, and you could see the brush marks in the finish if you looked close enough.

"No problem, Big Jim will fill the cans when you get back. Have a good one, Daniels." The old man nodded in reply. Rut smiled to himself as he climbed in and took his time unlocking his passenger door, ensuring that Daniels would have to come in very close proximity to Mango. The look on Mango's face through the passenger window was classic, a combination of panic, pain, and revulsion as Daniels climbed into his car. Mango started banging on the window.

"Unlock the damn door!"

"What? Oh, sorry about that, Mango." He unlocked the door and

Mango shot into the seat, closing the door immediately. By then Daniels was already backing out of his parking place.

"That old man's stink would gag a maggot! Don't he ever take a bath?"

"I couldn't tell you from firsthand knowledge, Mango. But I think he falls into the water once or twice a season. He lives out on Godwin Island, and claims his body odor keeps the biting flies and mosquitoes away. Besides, he gets all his water on the island from a cistern, which only gets filled with rainwater from the roof. He's careful not to waste it."

"In his case a bath wouldn't be a waste, it'd be a gift ta everybody that gets near him!"

Rut laughed, "He lives by himself on the island, so there's nobody around him most of the time to complain."

"Why do ya let him dock here?"

"Because he's not hurting anybody. He buys his fuel from me, and I let him park his car here. That guy knows more about these waters than anybody else you'll ever meet. See that marsh island?" Rut pointed out across Mockhorn Bay. "That's Mockhorn Island. He's got a narrow channel that cuts through it that he can run his Carolina Skiff through which nobody else would even dare to attempt. His island is on the other side of Mockhorn, right on the ocean. Been in his family for generations. He's got a shack there that's been built out of every kind of floating debris that he collected on the beach through the years. He's a very smart fellow, he's just a bit different and wants to be left alone. I kind of admire him; he lives life on his own terms."

"Yeah, an' in his own gas cloud. You ought to get your guys ta hose him down once in a while."

Typical, Rut thought. Mango wanted the world to conform to his own ideals, even those people in it that he had hardly any contact with at all, folks who weren't hurting him. He was beginning to think this lunch idea might not be such a good choice after all. He decided to redirect the conversation, "So, what's your target species in this tournament?"

"White marlin. Why?"

"You're lucky I spotted that cutlass bearing. Whites are very sensitive to noise like that. If you'd have gone out there with that shaft banging around like a bongo drum, you'd have never seen the first one. And what are you planning on using for bait?"

Mango replied, "Whatever they sell down at *Mallard Cove Marina*, that's where the tournament's out of. They got a bait shop there."

"Yeah, that's one of the best bait shops in the mid-Atlantic for frozen bait. But if you want to win or even be a contender, you're going to need live bait, which they don't sell. You'll need some Tinker mackerel."

Mango scowled, "So where can I get some uh those?"

"Well, you can catch them yourself, though that takes a lot of time to learn how. Or, you can buy some from the only bait guy I know who carries them, and he's your best bet."

"So, who's this guy?"

Rut had an evil grin, "You've already seen him."

"What's so funny? Who's the... No, you can't mean..."

"Yep. Daniels. Best live bait business around. If you want to win, you'll need to cut a deal with him before the tournament to be sure he has enough bait for you. Those live macks will make all the difference. I guarantee that all the top boats'll be using them."

Mango shuddered at the thought of being within smelling range of the man again. But if what Rut was saying was true, he'd be forced to. He was new at the tournament business, and there would be some heavy hitters fishing the *Mallard Cove White Marlin Open*. He wanted to make a good showing at it, and maybe even win the thing. He'd already hired the best freelance mate in Virginia Beach to fish it with him, and a few of his friends and associates were coming along, too. No way he wanted to be shown up in front of them.

"Okay, I guess I'll have to deal with him, but I'm at least gonna try and stay upwind."

Rut's grin got wider as he envisioned that transaction. "Smart move. It's the safe play."

"Yeah, just not for my sinuses."

# 2

## OVERDUE INTEREST

Rut and Mango took a table next to the beach at the open-air *Cove Beach Bar*. They looked out over the water as they waited on a server to bring them menus. Mango watched a couple out on a WaveRunner, showing off by doing dip turns while racing past, just offshore. They looked to be in their latter twenties. The man wasn't very toned, but the woman filled out every square inch of her tiny bikini very nicely indeed. Suddenly Mango's demeanor changed from enjoying watching them to becoming angrily fixated. Rut looked over at him, trying to figure out what had happened. He decided not to ask, at least not yet. Maybe she was an old girlfriend of Mango's and he was a jealous type; Rut didn't have a clue. Mango was closer to forty than thirty, and not bad looking. Rut had heard he had a reputation as somewhat of a "player" over in Virginia Beach, and that he liked younger women, so it's possible he might have known her. But players weren't generally the most jealous types.

Rut didn't have to wait long to find an answer to his unasked question as the WaveRunner made a beeline for the beach right in front of the bar. The guy gunned it right before they hit the shore, sliding it up on the sand a good five feet beyond the water, still showing off for the crowd in the bar. The pair dismounted the craft and Mango got up without a word and headed for the man. As he closed in on him the guy suddenly recognized Mango and went three shades whiter. He put his hands up as if to fend off Mango, and started backing up. The girl looked confused as her friend completely forgot about or ignored her, or both. Mango brushed past her, still intent on the guy who had now backpedaled well beyond his machine. Mango said something to him in a quiet voice that didn't carry all the way up to the bar. The girl started over to the two guys, but the guy held up a hand, then motioned for her to go on up to the bar.

The woman walked up the beach and stopped on the sand about ten feet from Rut, her attention focused on Mango and her friend. From where he sat, Rut could see that she was stunning. No doubt this was going to be one heck of a story when he got it all out of Mango. He continued watching the girl as well as the two men, the guy was now looking down, absentmindedly pawing the sand with a foot as Mango was talking. His head suddenly snapped up and shook side to side as Mango held his hand out, palm up. Whatever Mango said then completely deflated the guy, and he handed over something attached to a coiled orange plastic device. Rut had seen enough of them to know what it was even at this distance; he'd just surrendered the WaveRunner's key and kill switch. But after taking the key, Mango still held out his hand, and the guy began to argue. Finally, he handed over the wallet that he'd retrieved from a compartment in the WaveRunner. Mango removed some bills from it and handed it back to the guy. He looked like he was pleading with Mango who then hesitated and handed the guy two bills from the stack he'd taken.

As Mango headed back to the bar, the woman started down the beach to where her friend remained standing by himself, his head lowered, looking defeated. She shot a curious and slightly angry look at Mango as they passed each other. She reached her friend about the time Mango reached his chair and sat back down. Rut could see she wasn't getting an explanation that made her happy.

"What was that all about, Mango?"

"That was a guy who's late paying me back. He's been ducking me for two weeks, and now I see why. Instead of paying me like he was supposed to, he bought that water scooter thing to impress and get into the pants of that hottie. While I can understand he wasn't thinkin' 'cause he's an idiot and she's smokin' hot, that's somethin' I can't let go."

"So now he's all paid up."

"Of course not! Whatta I look like, a pawnbroker? That little water toy and the bankroll he had left that he was gonna use ta impress and keep beddin' that beach bunny don't even cover all the interest, not ta mention my inconvenience in havin' ta chase him. Hell, he's lucky I saw him now, 'cause it would've been a lot worse if one uh my guys had found him first. I already put a bounty out on him that woulda been added ta what he owes."

"So, he handed over the key and his wallet, just like that."

"Nah, he got a lot more sensible after I pointed out that it wasn't likely that she'd stick around and play nursemaid when he was laid up with two busted knees."

Rut was confused. "How did you expect him to work and pay you back if you break his knees?"

"First, I never said specifically that *I* was gonna break his knees; let's just say he just looks real accident prone ta me. Anyway, I ain't stupid enough ta loan money ta somebody who can't pay it back; you oughta know that from personal experience. That little geek never worked a damn day in his life. He's a trust fund kid, but his tail chasin' hobby has got him outspendin' the trust's income. That's why he came ta me for a 'bridge loan' ta get him through 'til he got his next cash distribution. He don't want his parents knowin' he was broke again. But the trust money came in and went right back out without payin' me. So now he's gonna have ta go ta Mommy and Daddy and explain that unless they want ta push him around in a wheelchair for the rest of the year, they'll need ta cough up what he owes, pronto."

Despite his original dealings over his loan from Mango, Rut had never really dwelled on all the mechanics of being a loan shark. He knew it could involve threats and intimidation, but now the whole violence thing had become all too real. It suddenly hit him that he was tied in with Mango with no foreseeable way of getting out of their deal unless he turned over his Miami contacts to him. Even then Mango might not let him totally out of it since he'd gotten used to Rut taking care of the deliveries, giving him half, and taking all the risks. Mango had just financed the first deals then provided a growing list of customers and supposedly that "protection." Rut had come to enjoy the cash their criminal enterprise generated, and giving up on it meant going back to getting by on what the boatyard brought in. Something he could do, albeit a bit reluctantly.

"Uh-oh." Mango had spotted the girl heading for their table with a determined look on her face. She walked up and addressed Mango.

"Kelly says you took all his money and our WaveRunner, Margo, and I want it back."

"The name is Mango, and he lied to you. Kelly owes me a bunch of money he was already supposed to have paid back."

"Margo, Mango, whatever. You're the one who's lying, because Kelly's rich." She said it proudly, like an angler who had just landed a citation-sized fish.

"Babe, you need ta ask yourself, if he's so rich why's he borrowing from me? Why did he beg me for that forty bucks I gave him since he said he was busted without it? He probably showed ya all his credit cards. I know you never seen him using one 'cause they're all maxed out. Kelly Roebuck ain't rich sweetheart, his *parents* are. Big difference. And last I heard they were good an' healthy, and not about to pay for his... habits. No matter how beautiful they might be."

Mango's explanation, coupled with a smile that even Rut had to admit was charming, was throwing the girl off her original mission to recover the money and the WaveRunner. She quickly rebounded and said, "We don't have any way to get back to Virginia Beach without the WaveRunner."

"I think you mean that you don't. Kelly already bolted with that forty."

She suddenly realized that Mango was right. Kelly was nowhere in sight, obviously wanting to avoid any further humiliation in front of her. "That son of a..."

Mango held up his hand. "Hold on now, uh, what didya say your name was?"

"I didn't. But it's Linda."

"Well, Linda, I'm about finished with my business here, an' I was about to move over ta the bar there and have some lunch. How's about you joining me, then we can run the WaveRunner over ta the boatyard where I have ta pick up my thirty-five-foot Ocean Yacht sportfisherman. I keep it over in Virginia Beach, and I'm taking it back there this afternoon. This way ya still get lunch an' drinks as well as a day out on the water, and I get your help handling my boat while I'm towing that thing." He motioned toward the beached machine.

"How do I know that you aren't some creepy rapist, or murderer or something?"

"Tell ya what, let's go sit at the bar and have that lunch an' talk. If after that ya don't wanna go, I'll pay for a ride-share ta take ya home."

"If I go with you, can I drive the WaveRunner? Kelly never let me drive."

"Absolutely." He stood up. "Thanks, Rut, I'll catch up with ya later, pal." He shot him a lascivious wink that the girl couldn't see as they started for the bar.

Rut shook his head slightly without even realizing it. Mango was nothing if not smooth. He guessed it came with the territory since the man was a hustler. He'd made his old Ocean Yacht sportfish sound like an actual *yacht* instead of the aging rig with run-out engines and soft, sagging decks that it was. Though he doubted Linda was all that savvy about boats; she would be impressed anyway.

"Eating by yourself this afternoon, Rut?"

He looked up to see a server he'd seen here several times before as she handed him a menu.

"It's looking that way... uh..."

"Cammie. Hey, sorry, I didn't mean to make you feel awkward. Angel told me your name."

He thought he detected a slight blush after she said that. Angel was another server here, and they'd dated a few times last year. Just fun and games, nothing serious since he'd been freshly divorced at the time. She eventually found a more permanent hook-up with a boat captain, and had been with him ever since. But she and Rut had remained casual friends.

"No, that's fine. I was just wondering where we might've known each other from."

"You've been in enough times since I started working here. Nice to finally put a name with a face."

He smiled. "It is at that."

"Hey, I'll let you look over the menu while I get your drink. What would you like?"

"Unsweetened iced tea with lemon. Thanks."

He watched as Cammie went to the bar to get his tea. She wore shorts that set off a very nice-looking pair of legs and anchored her hourglass figure. Even her loose-fitting *Mallard Cove* tee shirt couldn't camouflage her curves. Her wide shoulders gave way to shoulder-length light brown hair and a pretty face with hazel eyes. As far as he could tell she was probably somewhere a bit shy of forty, but she had one of those faces that never seemed to age. And she and Angel had been talking about him. Hmmm.

When she came back with his tea, she caught him checking her out. No blush this time, just a smile. A great smile. He tried to think of what to say to cover for it, but she spoke first.

"Here's your tea, Rut. Did you see anything you liked?"

"Uhhh, well..."

"On the *menu*." It was obvious that she was enjoying teasing him.

"Yeah, I'll have a seacake sandwich and fries."

"I'll get that right in for you." But she didn't seem to be in a hurry. "Angel and I are friends. Like I said, she was the one who told me who you were."

"Do I need to duck now?"

She laughed. It was a great laugh. "No. She said you are a good guy, and the two of you dated but didn't have the right chemistry for anything long-term."

"That's a good way to put it. She's still a good person though."

She nodded in agreement. "The reason I asked her about you was I have two tickets for the fishing tournament awards party and concert this Saturday night. It's already sold out and I was wondering if you'd like to use that second ticket. With me. Unless you're seeing somebody, or are busy, that's fine..."

"What, first you ask me to go with you, now you're trying to talk me out of it? Yes, I'd like to use that ticket. With you. Because I'm not seeing anybody, but I think I'd like to see you."

"Great! Do I pick you up, or you pick me up, or we can meet here..."

"Cammie, this is just a hunch, but by any chance did you just get out of some kind of long-term relationship?"

This time there was no mistaking the blush. "Is it that obvious?"

"Not at first, but you seem kind of nervous. Been there, done that, got the crappy tee shirt. So, I know how hard it can be." Rut smiled, trying to put her more at ease.

"I'm..."

"Like I said, nervous." He answered for her.

"Yes. Don't take this wrong, but Angel thought you would be a good first date for getting back out there. Well, that sure came out wrong." She looked embarrassed. "Speaking of coming out, you'll never get that seacake unless I get that order in." She left hurriedly.

"She's a real good person, Rut, but just a bit fragile right now." Angel had walked up beside him after being down at the beach, a favorite pastime on her day off. She too was in a bikini, but a less revealing one than Linda's. Fit, trim, and tan with sun-bleached hair, she stood about five feet, ten inches tall, and probably a couple of years older than Cammie.

"You told her I'd be a 'good first date' since she was getting back out in the dating world? What am I, training wheels?"

"You're a good guy who won't hurt her. Don't forget, I know you, inside and out. Otherwise, I'd have told her to steer clear of you."

"Thanks for that, I guess. I'd like to think I am, at least most of the time. Had lunch yet?" He motioned to Mango's vacated seat.

"I could do with a beer. That beach was hot, and I'm thirsty." She sat down. "I told Cammie I didn't think you were seeing anyone right now."

"Not lately. Been a bit busy. But she seems nice."

"She is. I think you two would be good together. You might even find the chemistry that we didn't."

"I haven't been looking for anything serious, Angel, you know that. But I'm glad that you found it with your guy."

"Me, too. But keep an open mind, she's a real good person. Just because you aren't looking for something doesn't mean you might not stumble into it. You're both stable people, which is something that's getting harder and harder to find in this world that's filled with all the crazy ones."

He nodded. "Run into my share of those."

"Haven't we all."

Rut looked over at the bar where Mango and Linda were sitting. She already had a hand on his arm and was laughing a bit too loud at his jokes. Yep, Mango was smooth. Definitely not one of the stable ones, but smooth. Angel followed his gaze.

"At least I thought you were stable." She looked back at him, frowning.

"Not what you think. I was watching my friend, not the girl."

She looked back over at the bar, then back at him. "Since when do you have such smarmy friends?"

"Okay, he's more of an acquaintance. We're working on his boat, and since I was headed out to lunch, I brought him along."

"And he went shopping," she replied.

"Here we are, Rut," Cammie said as she arrived with his order. "Hey, Angel. Bring you anything?"

"Hey, Cam. Kalik please."

"Coming up. Like anything else, Rut?"

"Nope, I'm good. Thanks, though."

After she left, Angel said, "See? That's what I mean. Smarmy dude over there probably would have had some creepy comeback when she asked what else you would like. I've heard 'em all. But you're polite and appreciative. Plus, if I remember right, you didn't rush me right into bed, and you did call me the next day like you said you would."

"Can we not talk about the past?" He looked worriedly over toward Cammie, who was headed back to their table.

"Don't worry, she knows all about that."

Rut rolled his eyes. "Of course she does."

"What? You think you guys are the only ones who brag or discuss these things with each other?" Angel was enjoying seeing Rut look so uncomfortable. "It's a rare thing these days to have a trustworthy friend who you used to see naked."

"I'll say." Cammie had reached their table and heard the tail end of the conversation. She set Angel's beer down in front of her.

"Great seacake, Cammie." Rut tried to change the direction of the conversation.

"It was great sex, Cammie." Angel grinned.

"Can we not?" Rut didn't like being outnumbered and outflanked.

"Of course we can't, my guy wouldn't appreciate us reliving old times, Rut."

"Angel, enough!"

"I don't recall you ever saying that back then." Both women laughed then Angel said to Cammie, "See what I mean? He's a good sport without being a *sport*."

"You sound like you're trying to sell a used car," Rut replied.

"Motorcycle. You're low mileage, and weren't ridden hard or often," she laughed again.

Cammie came to Rut's rescue by saying, "I have to get back to work. See you two later." She turned so that only Rut could see her and mouthed the words, "You're welcome."

Rut scowled at Angel. "What was all that about?"

"Just showing off your sense of humor and humility. Not that she wouldn't eventually see them, but now she'll feel more relaxed and comfortable on your date. Wouldn't you like to start off that way?"

"Maybe starting with a few more secrets would've been nice."

"Remember what I told you, women talk too."

"So I noticed."

"And you have a whole lot to talk about." She winked at him.

He ignored the comment and went back to work on his lunch but was interrupted when he saw Mango and Linda leaving. Mango gave him a nod and a thumbs-up as they passed by. That's when he saw a pretty blonde along with a stunning redhead walk into the bar and sit down two tables away from them. He'd seen the blonde in here before. Angel noticed him looking.

"The blonde is Lindsay Davis. She and her fiancé 'Murph' Murphy are the majority owners of this place. The redhead is Dawn Shaw. She and her husband Casey are also partners here. All of them are in together on a half dozen waterfront properties, including *Bayside Resort*."

Rut whistled softly. "That's some high-end real estate."

"Yeah, but they're regular people, and liveaboards here. I like working for them; they appreciate everything people do here."

Angel finished her beer, then said she had to run. "I'd say let me know how your date goes, but I'll probably already know by the time you figure it out." She grinned.

"No doubt."

AFTER LUNCH RUT was walking to the parking lot when he spotted the kid from this morning that had tried to sell him the electronics. It ticked him off that he hadn't taken his advice and left ESVA. And from the way he was scoping out all the boats from the docks, it was obvious he was casing the whole marina. Rut turned around and went back to the bar, and up to Lindsay and Dawn's table.

"Hi, sorry to interrupt y'all. My name is Sean Rutledge, I own a boatyard up on Mockhorn Bay." He pulled up the kid's picture on his phone, then showed it to them. "This kid's a boat burglar, and I ran him out of my place earlier today. He's out on your docks right now, casing the boats. Thought y'all should know it before your boats or your customers' boats get burglarized. Oh, and you need to be careful, the kid is fond of knives."

Lindsay asked, "Can I borrow your phone?" She sent the picture to

Murph's phone, then quickly texted the explanation for it from her own phone. He texted back that he was on it.

"Thank you, Mr. Rutledge, we appreciate the information," Dawn said.

"Just call me Rut. Glad I could help out."

Lindsay waved Cammie over. "Cammie, do we have any tickets left for Saturday's concert? I'd like to give Rut a pair of them."

"We don't, but that's covered since he's already going to it with me."

Lindsay looked surprised but said, "That's great! I didn't realize he was already a member of the '*Cove family*.' Put all your drinks for that night on my tab, and have fun. We'll see you there."

Cammie walked Rut out. "What was that about?"

"Tell you later. You can't know all my secrets before Saturday." It was his turn to grin.

"Okaaaay..."

"I'll call you later." She had left her number on his check.

"Yeah, I hear you're good about doing that." She laughed as she turned and went back to the bar.

After he got into his truck he got hit with a pile of mixed emotions. He was mad about the kid breaking into boats here in his area. He'd do whatever he had to in order to stop him. But suddenly he realized how he was part of the problem down in South Florida. By giving those thieves an easy way to sell their loot, he was enabling them. This had gone from being a way to get out from under Mango, to being a way to make easy money. It hadn't been that hard to justify continuing it, at least in his mind, because he never saw the thieves and the damage they caused. But now witnessing it happening in his own backyard, this put a different light on things. He felt like a real scumbag.

He had to get out of this, and he had to do it in a way that Mango would let him walk away without repercussions. As long as he was active in the business, he had Mango's umbrella of "protection." Once he was out of the business, that would no longer be available to him, if it ever truly was. In fact, he had no doubt he'd be expendable if Mango or his pals got to a point where they needed a fall guy.

Suddenly the kid went running past him, with two big guys in foot pursuit. The kid didn't recognize him, he was too busy trying to save his skin. Rut was now determined not to end up like him, running for his life. He was going to figure a way out before that happened.

# 3

## HONEST FRONT

That afternoon Rut was hard at work on his latest project, a thirty-year-old, twenty-nine-foot *Scarab* center console with twin outboards. It had looked like a good candidate for an artificial reef when he bought it, but his trained eye could see that it was structurally sound and only in dire need of cosmetics. He had been rebuilding and refurbishing boats for years; it had been a good source of side cash when he was married. With every boat sale, he had moved up to a larger and better boat for his next project, fixing each one and using it for a short while before moving on to the next. He had just sold an older forty-two-foot *Hatteras* sportfish when his wife left him, taking the contents of the house safe with her—a little over a hundred grand in cash. And that hit was even before her blood-sucking lawyer got started bleeding him. He hated lawyers.

In Virginia, all boats are taxed each year based on their valuation. It's easier to get a lower valuation when you have a recent bill of sale that reflects that number and helps you establish a lower base. Rut offered many of his buyers paperwork that reflected a lower selling price if they would make up the difference in cash, which went into that safe at his house. The one his wife cleaned out. And which he couldn't claim in the divorce without opening himself up for charges of tax evasion. She knew there was nothing he could do about it, and ironically, the retainer for her lawyer came out of this stash.

It wasn't until Rut got into the deal with Mango that he made enough cash to start this side business again. With the majority of the boatyard's business being commercial workboats which receive only the most meager cosmetic maintenance, his refurbishing business fed his more artistic side, allowing him to bring these boats back to their original luster. The money that it generated was nice, but almost more importantly these days it fed a hunger, a true need of his soul. It helped replenish his sense of self-worth that had left, along with his wife. There was just something about looking at a refurbished boat that he once again took pride in, knowing it got back to that point through the use of his own two hands.

"Hey, Rut, you around?"

He stood up, having been out of sight, lying on his side while sanding the gunwales of the *Scarab*, prepping them for paint. "Oh, hey Rev. Over here."

Eddie "Rev" Jones, a former waterman turned preacher at the *Waterman's Church of ESVA*, was standing at the edge of the boatyard, looking around. He spotted Rut and walked over to the boat which was on its trailer in front of Rut's house, which was also part of the boatyard. Rev climbed the stepladder that was next to the boat, then sat on a covering board.

Rev commented, "This one's a blast from the past."

"Yeah, I've wanted one since I was a kid. These were tops on the 'cool list' back when I was a teenager."

This particular model of *Scarab* was completely open, without a cabin. Everything about it was sleek and swept back, looking like a "go fast" boat crossed with a center console fishing rig, taking the best features of both and combining them. The tee-top supports were even raked back to give the feel of speed, a real rarity in the day, though it has become a more common design, now some decades later. The *Scarab's* deep-vee hull gives it the smoothest ride in almost any sea, though it lacks a little stability when trolling in the trough of a beam sea.

"Looks like you're giving this one the full treatment, as always."

"Wouldn't know how else to do one, Rev. I've got a reputation to uphold."

"Yeah, you do. And your reputation is what I came over to talk to you about." He paused a minute, seemingly searching for the right way to approach what he wanted to say. "That was a good thing you did for Andy today." Not much happened around the commercial fishing community on ESVA that Rev didn't eventually hear about.

"That 'come here' really pissed me off, stealing from him. I was just glad to help."

"Like you did with Freddy Vaca, getting him back in business out on the water. Even though all that gear you practically gave him was hot enough to fry an egg on."

Rut slowly got up off the deck then hopped up onto the lean seat, looking at his friend. "I don't know what you mean, Rev. I was just helping out one of my customers when he was down. I thought that's what the good book said I'm supposed to do."

"It does. But it also says not to steal, nor bear false witness."

"I don't steal. And I don't put up with anyone who tries pulling that crap around here, like that kid." He avoided doubling down his denial.

Rev sighed. He and Rut had known each other their whole lives, and they both knew that they could trust each other. "You know I did a little bit of that when I was younger, before I heard the calling that led me to the church. But you were always the straight shooter, so honest and hard working. At least up until Debbie left. Though you seem to be getting back on your feet now, and that's great news. But some things are getting back to me that are... concerning."

If they didn't have the common history that they shared, Rut would've told Rev to pound sand and get the hell off his boat. But he knew Rev wasn't sticking his oar in his business just to be a busybody. Though Rut wasn't a member of his or any other church, he knew Rev was doing what he felt was the right thing.

"What are you hearing?"

"That you're tied in somehow with that loan shark from across the bridge—Mango. That you were seen with him at the *Cove* today."

"He's a customer. We went to lunch while his boat was being worked on."

Rev held up a hand, "That may well be, but just being seen with the guy is guilt by association. I heard he even made a collection there, in full view of a packed lunch crowd. Sean, like you said yourself, you've got a reputation to uphold, and it's not just about refurbishing boats." It had been years since Rev had used Rut's given name, so he knew how worried the preacher was. "And Freddy Vaca has been running his mouth that you're selling hot electronics. I think he thinks he's helping you, and by doing it he's trying to repay how you helped him."

Rut started to object, but again Rev held up a hand. "I don't want to know if it's true or not, and I don't want you to feel like you have to lie to me again. We've never done that before to each other over the years, and I don't want either of us to make it a habit now. I'm just doing you a favor by telling you what I'm hearing. Because if I'm hearing it, you can be sure it's getting around to people who might use it as a bargaining chip if they were to get busted. I'm not telling you so you'll watch your stern, I'm telling you as a friend so that if you are involved with something like that, you need to get out of it while you can. You've made some great strides in your life since Debbie left, so don't make one of the biggest mistakes now that you could. Remember, you've never been to jail, and I have. You don't want to go there. Jail is bad enough, but I've heard prison is a thousand times worse. Nothing is worth that."

Rut just sat silently on the seat, trying to process everything that he'd just heard—the nightmare he'd just heard. Now Mango wasn't his biggest concern, though wait, he was now an even *bigger* concern. When Mango heard that Rut's part of the business had been exposed, Rut had no illusions as to what Mango would be capable of doing in order to protect himself. As Rut had already figured out, he was expendable.

"Thanks for coming over, Rev. I'll keep what you told me in mind."

Rev nodded, understanding that the "non-denial, denial" confirmed what he'd heard that had brought him here. While Rut wasn't an official member of his congregation, as an old friend, he still counted him as a member of his flock. He hoped he'd just helped to save his butt, and at some point he hoped to save his soul. One thing at a time though...

∼

"So, tell me why isn't this a state case?" FBI Special Agent Stephanie Baker was surprised that this one had been handed off to her. She was temporarily assigned as an investigator for the US Attorney's office in Norfolk.

Assistant US Attorney Ron Devaro frowned, he was irritated at being second guessed by a lowly FBI agent. "Because I want this guy, and because I can tie him to a RICO count; Racketeer Influenced and Corrupt Organization Act. He supposedly forced one of his borrowers to hand over businesses in two states. That, and the fact that he has threatened the son of Edward Roebuck, after the boy didn't make his payments on time. I want this 'Mango' son of a bitch off my streets. And I need you to dig and find out everything you can about him so I can put him away and weld the door shut on his cell. So get going and give me more to work with! I want to get his case in front of my new Grand Jury when it convenes the first week of next month."

Neither had noticed the office assistant who had been hovering around Devaro's open office door, but she had heard everything. She'd keep her eyes and ears open, and pass it along.

# 4

## CHANGES

The next day Rut called Big Jim into the office. Jim sat in the chair across from him as he explained what happened. "I've got a little problem. Rev came to see me last night; he's hearing things around ESVA about my distribution business. Said that if he is hearing about it, then it won't be long before someone else will who might use that kind of information to save their own skin. As much as I hate to do it, I've got to shut it down. Jim, I know that you've come to rely on the extra cash."

Jim stopped him, "Naw, that's all I ever thought it was, Rut, extra cash. Meanin' I knew it could dry up any time. Ain't worth goin' to jail over. In fact, I was gonna talk to you this mornin'. I think Vaca ran his mouth too much, and you can't put that cork back in the bottle. Rev's right, it ain't a question of *if* word gets back to the wrong people, but more like *when*. May have already. I think you're a smart man to put an end to this stuff."

"I'd have been a smarter man not to have done any of it at all. I know Mango's not going to be happy about me getting out."

"Yeah. There's him to deal with. Maybe if you give him the info on the Miami man, he may leave you alone?"

"I don't know, Jim. I think he always had it in the back of his mind that if anything happened, he'd just throw me to the law and walk away clean. With his contacts, he could probably get away with it too. But like you said, he doesn't want any entanglements either. We just shipped out that last load, and it'll be next month before Miami can put together another one. That'll let me pick my time between now and then to break it to him. Timing is everything. He's got that tournament this weekend, and if he lucks out and catches a few, he'll be in a good mood for a while."

"Let's hope the fishing gods are on his side then."

"Yeah."

∼

Rut had a lot on his mind, and he wanted to get away from the boatyard over lunch. He wondered if Cammie was working today, and decided to find out. Since it was midweek, the *Cove Beach Bar* wasn't that busy, and she was one of the few servers on this shift. She looked bored, but quickly brightened up when she saw him.

"Hey! Two days in a row, Rut, that's a new record for you."

He liked that she had been keeping count, since she'd obviously been watching him for a while. He mentally kicked himself for not noticing her first, and not having been the one to ask her out, instead of the other way around. "Yeah, I really like the food here." He smiled, and she laughed.

"I'm glad it keeps you coming back. I was hoping I'd get to see you again before the concert," she said.

"You're not backing out, I hope."

"What? No! I was just thinking it would be nice to get a chance to see you again and talk. It's probably going to be loud around here on Saturday."

"Kind of hard to talk much while you're working."

"True. I get off at four though. What are you doing around then?"

"I've got this boat I'm working on."

She looked confused, "No, I mean after work."

"So do I. It's a side project. I love taking old boats and making them look new again."

"Then I'd love to see it."

"Well, come over after you get off. My house is in the northeast corner of the boatyard, and my boat is right in front of the house."

"I'll be there. Now, what can I get for you?"

∽

RUT WAS glad Cammie was coming over. She was right about the awards party and concert; it was going to be loud with the band playing as well as all the boat owners and crews getting liquored up. Not a great place to get to know someone, especially when you're skittish, as he assumed she might be. She seemed nice enough, but this situation might quickly get sticky if he wasn't careful. If things didn't go well and it was perceived as his fault, Angel wasn't going to be happy. He was particularly proud of the fact that the two of them had parted amicably and remained friends. It was testimony to the fact that he'd hit that age where he had matured beyond the point of all the drama. He wasn't sure how happy Angel's new beau was about them being friendly, but at least the guy was confident enough in himself to more or less ignore it.

Rut was back to lying on his side on the deck, sanding the gunwales when a six-pack of *Starr Hill Northern Lights IPA* suddenly appeared on the covering board. A second later Cammie's grinning face appeared behind it.

"Hope you don't mind; I brought some beer for when you want to take a break. It's from my hometown of Crozet, over by Charlottesville."

"*Starr Hill*! I love their beer." Cammie had just moved a notch higher on Rut's list. Not only had she thought to bring beer, but she brought a great India Pale Ale. He knew that you could tell a lot about a person by their choice of beer. Had she shown up with a "suitcase" of "*Natty Light*," he'd have known she was more into guzzling "session beers." But a six-pack of such a great IPA showed that she drank more for flavor, and he liked that about her. This wasn't a beer that you chugged. "So, you're from Crozet. I spent a weekend over there once, hitting the wineries."

She looked surprised, "I don't remember you ever ordering wine at the *Cove*." She climbed into the boat, sitting on the covering board.

Again he was reminded that she apparently had been watching him for a while. "It wasn't my idea; it was my ex's." He mentally kicked himself now for having mentioned the trip.

She nodded, "That's where I left my ex, so I won't be going back there any time soon." She looked around the *Scarab*, now anxious to change the subject. "This is such a cool rig! Vintage design, but it was so far ahead of its time when this model was produced."

Now it was Rut's turn to be surprised. "You know your boats."

"My dad had outboards, and we used to go out on the Chesapeake a lot of weekends when I was growing up."

"Maybe we passed each other on the water back then," Rut said.

"It's possible. Ready for a break and a beer?" She also seemed to want to steer back away from stories about the past.

"Twist my arm," he grinned and held out a hand.

After passing him a beer and opening one for herself, she held up the can, "To new friends."

"Who bring beer!" he replied, tapping his can against hers.

She said, "There's an old saying, the way to please a woman is to miss football in order to take her to dinner, but the way to please a man is to... uh... bring beer."

She looked chagrinned, and Rut knew why. She'd started quoting the saying before realizing everything it included.

"Um, you kind of left a bit of that out. It's '...*show up naked*, and bring beer.'" He laughed as she blushed.

"I remembered that part after I started quoting it. Sorry, you'll have to get by with only being halfway pleased."

"Oh, I'd say I'm pretty pleased. You're funny as hell, Cammie."

She beamed. "My friends call me Cam."

"Cam it is then."

She looked relieved that he'd chosen to give her an out instead of continuing to tease her about the misquote. "Well, I guess we both broke one of the big rules about getting to know someone by bringing up our exes. And that quote, well, I don't know you nearly well enough to have used that one."

Rut chose to sidestep the part about their exes, "Hey, you didn't just bring beer, you brought *great* beer. That makes up for the other part. Almost." He chuckled.

"Angel said you have a great sense of humor, and she wasn't kidding."

"She didn't leave much to your imagination about me, did she?"

Cammie shook her head and smiled, "Nope. It's funny, you're the only, uh, past boyfriend that she talks about and is still on good terms with. See how I avoided saying that whole 'ex' thing there?"

"Very clever, Cam." He paused then said, "It's funny, I never thought of her as a girlfriend, or me as her boyfriend. We were just very close friends, period."

"With very hot benefits, from what she said."

"You'd have to talk to her about that."

"She already talked to me, but she told you that part."

He sighed and looked serious. "Yeah. Hey, so she had already been talking to you about me before you decided you wanted to ask me to the concert thing?"

"What, do you think it was her idea? Yes, we'd talked about a guy named Rut, but I didn't know that was you then. So no, it wasn't her idea, it was mine, and she wasn't 'fixing me up.' Until that point, I hadn't put two and two together since I didn't know you were... you. But once I did, she pushed me like a bulldozer."

"Sorry, I keep thinking about her saying I'd be a good first date for you to get back into dating. Got to tell you, I'm really not into the idea of being a stepping stone. I like to know what to expect beforehand."

"I wish I'd never told you that part. But you know how she's like a mother hen to her friends."

Rut nodded, "Oh, believe me, I know. That's one of the things that I like about her, except when it comes to me."

"Understood. I don't use people Rut, especially not in the way that sounded. And for the record, I'm not much on being pushed into things by other people, either. But she's right you know."

"About what?"

"You are a great first date. I'm counting this as a date since there's beer involved. And as far as 'getting back out there,' I am looking forward to it. At least by going on date number two. With you. I was really nervous about this, but you're easy to be around and talk to. You don't pull punches, and so far you don't seem like the type of guy to play head games."

"I treat people the way I want to be treated. I've been on the receiving end of that crap before, and I don't have the time or patience for it or anybody who does."

She raised her can again, "I'll drink to that." After they clinked cans she asked, "Is there somewhere I can put the rest of these to stay cold?"

"My refrigerator in the kitchen. The door's unlocked."

She returned a few minutes later and smiled and said, "Are you sure you aren't seeing anyone? I've never seen a bachelor's place so neat and clean before."

"Nope, but I can't take the credit. The wife of one of my customers does housecleaning, and she was here today. He's a commercial fisherman, and they really need the extra money. Works out well for all of us."

Cammie cocked her head slightly and said, "You're a good man, Rut."

"Oh, don't judge me too fast, Cam, you're just getting to know me."

"I'm enjoying doing it, too."

Rut handed her some sandpaper. "I'm guessing since you grew up around boats, you know how to work with this. And if you want to ride around on this rig when she's done, you've got to hold up your end in the meantime."

"I figured there was a chance of becoming a conscript, that's why I changed into these clothes after work. Though this wasn't exactly what I had in mind when Angel told me that you really know how to treat a girl." She grinned. "But you know what? I'm glad I came over."

"I'm glad you did, too. You really get to know someone when you work on a project boat together."

"Did you and Angel ever work on a boat together?"

"I thought she told you every little detail of our time together."

"Mostly just the sex and the dinners out. You know, the good parts, not the manual labor." She laughed when she saw him grimace.

"Well, then for the record, no, she and I never worked on a project together. This is the first boat I've had since my divorce; I didn't have one during the short period that Angel and I spent time together. And that's my last answer to any question about Angel, okay? I don't want to get into the habit of having anything I do now compared to anything I did with her back then."

"Who said I was also going to do anything with you that you also did with her?"

"I was already planning on asking you something, and I had you figured for an 'easy yes.' But if you don't want to, then I won't bother to ask."

She put her sandpaper down, her hazel eyes now flashing with anger and indignation. "Oh, you thought I was easy, did you? I thought Angel said you didn't rush her into bed." The volume of her voice now increased with her anger. "What makes you think I'm different? That I'd be more willing to jump right into the sack with you? Just because Angel said y'all were great together doesn't mean I'm in any hurry to find out for myself if we would be. She never told me you had such a huge ego."

Rut said quietly, "What I was planning on asking you was if you'd go to dinner with me at *Rooftops Grille at Bayside Resort*. That's what I'd hoped would be an 'easy yes.' A third date as a 'thank you' for the concert, and for wanting to help me with my boat. I thought I was being funny the way I was asking, but I screwed it up. I didn't mean to make you mad. Sorry."

His explanation sunk in and she said, "Oh. I'm sorry, too. I guess I was comparing how you and she were..."

"Which is exactly why I wanted to avoid questions about her. And comparisons." He shrugged.

"Maybe I had better go."

"You haven't finished sanding that section yet, conscript. How do you expect to still get invited to dinner if you don't finish your job?"

She went back to sanding, the redness in her face and ears from the anger and embarrassment slowly fading. "About that dinner invitation, you're right, I'm easy. About that. I'd really like to go there with you, if you're still asking."

"Nope. You see, you're wrong. The last thing in the world that you are is 'easy.' Gun-shy, nervous, and properly cautious, those are all much better words to describe you. But yeah, I'm still asking."

# 5

## SAND DANCERS

*Saturday afternoon...*

THE *MALLARD COVE MARINA* parking lot was jammed when they arrived, so Rut and Cammie ended up parking way down past the bait shop near the tree line at the property edge. Even that far away they could hear the music coming from the *Driftwood Stage* over on the beach when they stepped out of the truck. Murph and Lindsay had hired one of the best bands in the mid-Atlantic for the party. They played "yacht rock" and islands music with a slight country twang that the sportfishing crowd loved. Cammie grabbed his hand and pulled Rut along faster, like a little kid who was excited to get to the county fair. As they finally queued up in the line to get their tickets exchanged for wristbands, Cammie started swaying to the music.

"I hope you like to dance, Rut, I forgot to ask you about that. I love it."

"I can hold my own, I guess. My dancing gets better in proportion to how much alcohol I've had, or that you've had."

She laughed and put both hands on his hips, as she was now in full dance mode. She was smiling and moving to the beat and he couldn't help but join in.

"Not bad! And you haven't even had a drink yet," she said.

He suddenly realized he was grinning, his smile matching hers. He'd already seen her laugh and smile, but now there was more depth to it. Her love for life and living was showing, in a big way. She saw the way he was looking at her. "What?" She was still grinning.

"Just seeing a new side to you."

"That's because you've only seen me when I was at work, and then when I dropped by your place, where you also put me to work," she kidded him.

"Well, that's true. But I liked that side too."

"There's a time for work, Rut, and a time to play. I don't do either one halfway."

"I've kinda forgotten how to do that second part lately. I'm glad you asked me to come out with you tonight."

She looked at him as if studying his face for the first time, her smile fading a little before quickly returning. "Then it's high time you remembered how."

They got their wristbands at the gate that had been set up across the breezeway entrance that led to *Mallard Cove's* two beach bars. Then she took him by the hand again, weaving their way through the crowd out onto the beach in front of the stage. He couldn't help but look at her, from her loose and flowing bare midriff top to her boat shorts, and her firm, tan legs. Leather flip-flops and a beaded leather anklet rounded out her perfect beach-party look. She turned and smiled as she saw him looking, then put her hands on his shoulders as she started dancing again. The dancing became their means of communication as it was way too loud for voices to be heard above the band. He was glad they'd had the time to talk the other day at his house.

After two more songs, the band took a break long enough for Murph and Lindsay to start handing out the awards. Much to Rut's surprise, Mango and his crew took third place. As they trooped happily across the stage to pick up both their trophy and check, he saw that Linda was with Mango, in an even smaller bikini than she'd worn the other day. Rounding out his crew was the freelance mate from Virginia Beach and his girlfriend, and a couple of guys that looked like, and probably were, some of his "leg-breakers." Each of them was accompanied by a skimpily attired girl, and all of the women looked like they were straight out of one of the strip joints from over across the bridge.

"Isn't that your friend?" Cammie asked.

"Customer, not friend. And yeah, that's him. Hey, let's go get some drinks." He wanted to both change the subject as well as avoid running into Mango. On the way to the bar Cammie and Rut were spotted by Dawn Shaw, who was sitting at a table in the *Catamaran Bar* along with her husband. She beckoned the two of them over.

Dawn said, "Casey, of course you know Cammie, and this is Sean Rutledge. He pointed out that boat burglar the other day."

Casey Shaw stood and smiled at Cammie before saying hello, then offered his hand to Rut who shook it and said, "Please call me Rut."

"Rut it is then. You guys want to sit down? Angel is running drinks." Several of the tables had been removed, allowing more room for walk-up business at both the *Catamaran* and the *Cove Beach Bar* during the event. Most of the remaining tables were reserved for good customers and friends.

Rut looked over at Cammie, who nodded. "Sure, thanks."

As if on cue, Angel appeared, looking at Cammie and raising a questioning eyebrow even before asking what she and Rut were drinking. Then she headed off in the direction of the service bar.

Rut said, "Thank you both, you just saved us twenty minutes of standing in line."

Dawn replied, "And you saved us a lot of trouble, pointing out that kid who was casing the place. I don't think he'll be coming back around here again, thanks to Murph."

"Was this what you wouldn't tell me about the other day?" Cammie asked, and Rut nodded.

"The kid was scoping out some boats. I'd already run him out of my place a couple of hours earlier."

"What a creep. I'm glad you saw him. Boat thieves are the absolute lowest." She saw Rut almost wince, but quickly recover, and she wondered why.

Rut changed the subject. "I understand that you two are live-aboards here."

Casey said, "We're actually in a little cove just beyond the trees at the end of the parking lot. Us and a handful of our friends. We'll have to have you over some time."

"I'd like that, thanks."

Cammie gave Rut an appreciative look over the way that he'd obviously befriended both of the Shaws so quickly. It seemed that they had also surprised each other; Cam for her dancing, and Rut for having a hand in preventing crime. Their drinks soon arrived, followed soon afterward by Murph and Lindsay. Rut recognized Murph as one of the guys who had run after the kid, which explained Dawn's comment. Lindsay recognized Rut, and introduced him to Murph.

Rut liked both couples, who didn't seem the least bit put off to be socializing with a server from one of their restaurants, as so many other owners might have been. In fact, if you didn't know who they were, at first glance you might not think that any of them had two dimes to rub together. You certainly wouldn't figure them for being partners in several of the most lucrative businesses and properties around the Chesapeake. Rut and Cammie hung out and talked with them for a few more minutes until the band cranked back up, then they were back on the beach, once again dancing in the sand.

THE BAND WAS NOW FINISHED, and the bars were again lined up with thirsty patrons. Many of those who had attended the concert had now gone over to the *Cove Restaurant* and the *Fin and Steak*, the other two eateries in the *Mallard Cove* complex. Both were mobbed, with long waiting lines in front of each. Cam and Rut then decided to go out for pizza at a great little hole-in-the-wall joint about fifteen minutes north. As they walked through the marina, they heard a commotion out on one of the floating docks. As they reached the ramp that led down to it, they saw Dawn loudly arguing with some goon who was very drunk and belligerent. There was no mistaking Dawn's mane of bright red hair, even at that distance. The man's female companion was sitting on the dock, one side of her face beet red from being hit with an open hand. Dawn must've seen this happening, and decided to intervene.

Rut and Cam raced down the ramp and out on the dock to help Dawn. But what came next shocked them both as the man shoved Dawn. She lost her balance and fell off the dock, hitting her head against the stern of the boat occupying that slip. By the time they reached the spot where she'd gone over the side, she had already sunk just below the surface. Rut dove in, and grabbed one of her arms. He pulled her unconscious form over to where Cam could help him haul her up onto the dock. They turned her onto her side, and she began to cough up water as she regained consciousness. Casey had been a minute behind them and now came running up.

As Casey and Cam attended to Dawn, Rut now looked for the goon who had shoved her, but he and the girl had disappeared. Then he spotted Mango's boat, *Mangoritaville*, making its way out the marina basin's inlet. Putting two and two together, Rut figured the man who shoved Dawn must've been one of Mango's henchmen, even though he hadn't gotten a good look at him. But that would explain Mango not wanting to stick around and wait for the law to start asking questions.

Rut went back to the trio saying, "Those two disappeared. Must've left on a boat. Are you okay, Dawn?"

"Yes, thanks to you two, and having a thick skull. My head's kind of throbbing though."

"C'mon, we'll get you to the emergency room," Casey said.

"I don't need to go to the emergency room, I'm fine. I know what day and year it is and I'm not puking anymore, so I don't have a concussion. I just want to go back to the boat."

Casey knew better than to argue with her, he'd just watch her closely and if she showed any symptoms of a concussion, he'd get her to the hospital right away. He helped her stand up, then he and Cam walked on either side of her, with Rut bringing up the rear. They walked past the boat in-and-out storage barn, and over to the tree line. Rut now saw there were two gates in the fence, one vehicle sized, and the other obviously for pedestrians, each with a keypad. Both entryways curved through a narrow but thick evergreen wood that prevented anyone from seeing what lay beyond it. Casey punched in a code, opening the walk-through gate for all of them.

The woods gave way to a covered L-shaped parking area that bordered a small private marina with a handful of boats. They were various types, from center console outboards and multi-deck houseboats, to a 110-foot Hargrave yacht on the far end which they were apparently headed for. As they all went up the gangway, Rut saw the name-board on the side of the salon read *Lady Dawn*—a stunning yacht named after a beautiful woman.

Once Dawn was safely wrapped in a towel and seated in the cavernous salon, Rut said "Well, I'm glad you're fine, Dawn. We just wanted to help make sure you got home okay."

"I can't thank you two enough. But you can't go anywhere without having a drink first, I insist. Consider it a down payment on what I owe both of you."

"You don't owe us anything, and I'm dripping all over your carpet. I'm going to go home and get changed, then we're going out for pizza."

Dawn said, "In that case, you can take 'to-go' drinks with you, along with a raincheck for a night when you both are free and can come back to have dinner and drinks."

Casey went over to a beautiful granite-topped bar and asked what each of them was drinking. He filled two plastic glasses that were printed with "*Lady Dawn*" on the sides. Then he walked the two of them out to the dock.

"Thank you both again. If you hadn't been there..." He didn't have to finish that sentence; they knew what he was thinking.

"Don't mention it, Casey, I'm just glad we were, and that Dawn's okay," Cammie said.

She and Rut walked slowly toward the gate path, sipping their cocktails and taking in what little they could see of the private compound in the dark. Cammie asked Rut, "Do you think they meant it about coming back another time for dinner?"

"I get the feeling from those two that they're pretty straight shooters, so yes, I do."

She wove her arm through his as they walked along. "Angel was wrong, you know."

Rut turned his head to look at her in the low light. "About what?"

"You being a good step for 'getting back out there.' You're a lot more than that. Look how much you charmed the Shaws. And I don't know how many people I know who would've dived in after Dawn in that dark water."

"Probably more than you know. Heck, I didn't know for sure myself that I would until I did. Never really stopped to think about it before I jumped in."

"That's what I'm talking about. You're a good guy."

He sighed heavily as he stopped, thinking about what she'd said earlier about boat thieves. If she knew about his side business, he had no doubt that she'd get as far away from him as fast as she could. It only strengthened his resolve to cut his ties soon with Mango and that business. "The thing is, you don't know everything there is to know about me, Cam."

She laughed, "And I wasn't planning to, since it's only our second date. Though you're pretty charming, in a not-so-smarmy kind of way. And a pretty good dancer." She poked him lightly in the ribs with a finger.

He realized that she was so easy to talk to that if he wasn't careful, he might slip and mention something about his past illegal activities. The ones that he was now done with. It felt good, knowing he was putting that part of his life behind him, especially after the way she had reacted on learning about that kid who was casing the place. He'd only gotten into that business because of his divorce, at least that's how he was rationalizing it to himself. If he'd not been put into such a tight cash squeeze, he'd never have gotten involved with Mango. Then there'd never have been any need to get involved in selling stolen stuff. So, in a way it was all his ex's fault, right?

Who was he kidding... a truly honest man might have been tempted, but would have never followed through on it. The truth was he'd jumped at the chance. He could've stopped after that second deal and walked away, with Mango paid off and out of his life. But he hadn't. There were vintage song lyrics that spoke about the lure of easy money having such a strong appeal. But appealing didn't even come close. For him, it had been almost a narcotic, and now it was time to quit, "cold turkey," before he ended up behind bars. He had a growing reputation as a good guy, and it was high time to start earning it...

"Hello? Earth to Rut?"

He suddenly realized he'd been standing silently still, ignoring Cammie without meaning to. He refocused on her face just as she kissed him.

"Wow, what did I do to earn that?" he asked.

She grinned, "I thought the reason you went all silent on me was you were getting up your courage to do that. So, I figured I'd go ahead and do it myself, rather than wait on you."

"Weren't you supposed to be skittish about getting back into dating? Yet you asked me out, and then you kissed me..."

"Well, apparently you hadn't thought about asking me first, and I figured you were lagging again."

"No, I was just thinking about something."

"You think too much." She leaned forward and kissed him again.

# 6

## THE SUMMONS

On Monday Rut arranged to meet Mango at the *Catamaran* bar for lunch. It was the less busy of the two beach bars at lunchtime, and they could have a little privacy without having to meet completely in private, which would make what he had in mind a bit tougher. With a few people sitting nearby, Mango could get neither loud nor violent when Rut gave him the news. Neither was a certainty, but he knew Mango wouldn't be happy. Rut got there ahead of time, picking out his table carefully, with the adjacent ones vacant. Fortunately, both Angel and Cammie were working next door at the *Cove*, and wouldn't see what was going to happen.

Rut felt a hand on his back and looked up to see Dawn standing over him. "I want to thank you again for rescuing me the other night."

"Don't mention it, Dawn. I'm willing to bet you would have done the same thing."

"Probably, even though we don't really know each other. I guess you never know for sure what you'll do until you're faced with that situation. By the way, Casey and I were serious about having you and Cammie over for dinner. Why don't you talk it over with her, see what night works best for you guys and give us a call." She handed over her card, which he glanced at and then pocketed.

"Thanks, I'll do that."

Unfortunately for Rut, Dawn took the nearest two-top table. She then started to shuffle through a small stack of mail. Lindsay arrived and took the seat across from her.

"The scenery just keeps getting better around here." Mango had walked up as Dawn left, apparently unaware that Dawn was the one his leg-breaker had attacked, if he knew about it at all. He was now scoping out both women.

"Mind your manners if you want to keep coming here, Mango. One's married, the other is engaged. They own this joint, and they live here."

Mango scowled at Rut just as they heard Dawn exclaim, "Aw, damn! I've got jury duty Linds, *federal grand jury* duty. Three days a month for a whole *year*!" She was holding a letter she'd just opened, along with a pamphlet titled, Handbook for Federal Grand Jurors.

Mango's ears perked up as he strained to hear what else she might say.

"Every first Wednesday, Thursday, and Friday of the month at the federal courthouse over in Norfolk. I've never heard of having to serve for a full year before. That's thirty-six days. Damn it!"

Lindsay replied, "Well, that should be it for a few years then."

"It damn well better be."

Rut could see the gears turning in Mango's head, and it worried him. He had originally planned on discussing their business after they ate, but now he figured it might be a good idea to go ahead and distract him with it. He slid an envelope across the table with the contact information of their Miami supplier.

Mango looked down at the envelope. "What's this?"

Rut kept his voice low enough so that he couldn't be overheard by Dawn or Lindsay, "The info on that Miami supplier. I'm out."

Mango lifted his head, giving Rut a blank look. "Whatta ya mean you're out?"

"I mean, I'm done. Going back to legit. I don't want anything to do with selling hot stuff anymore, if you want to keep going, that's all on you."

Mango quickly glanced around then said, "Keep your voice down. An' there's no getting out unless I say so, an' I don't."

"You don't have any choice. I had a little problem. A guy I helped out thought he was doing me a favor by telling some other folks about it, and now the word is out."

"Damn it! Why'd ya go an' do something dumb like that? Did this guy know about my end?"

"No, he only knew about me. I talked to him and he's forgotten all about it already."

Mango was now looking at Rut like he was radioactive. "Yeah, well you just forget all about me."

"My problem is that I'm not sure you'll forget about me, Mango."

Mango glanced down and to his right, "I don' know whatcha mean." That little glance told Rut everything he needed to know; it was a lie.

"You know exactly what I mean. To you, I'm a loose end. And loose ends normally get tied up. But not this one. I've got an insurance policy, and so long as I stay healthy, your name stays out of the papers and off the DA's desk. But anything happens to me, and the roof'll cave in on you."

"You sonofa..."

"Just be cool. Like I said, all I want is out."

CAMMIE HAD COME over to the bar to get some limes for her bartender since the *Beach Bar* had run out. She was surprised to see Rut was here at the *Catamaran* since he hadn't even stopped by next door to say hello. She started to walk over to his table when she noticed he was in an argument with that guy who he had said was a customer. The whole thing had a weird vibe to it so she retreated to the bar, grabbed her limes then went back over to the other bar, wondering what it was about. And wondering where things now stood with Rut and her, since it looked like he was intentionally avoiding her.

. . .

MANGO GLARED at Rut and stood up, clutching the envelope. Without another word he left, scanning the faces in the bar as he did. Five minutes later a man got up from his seat at the bar, then made his way over to Rut's table, taking the seat Mango had vacated.

Rut asked, "Did you get it?"

Rev grinned and held up the cell phone he'd used to video Rut's meeting from across the room in high definition with its telephoto lens. "You betcha. How about you?"

Rut smiled, removing the tiny microphone from under his shirt. A wire ran from it to Rut's cell, where the audio of the meeting had been recorded. "Between what we both got, it's enough to fry him if he messes with me in any way." He paused and sighed, "For the first time since Debbie left me, I feel totally free. I've gotten my business as well as my life back, and I owe you a great deal for helping me with that, Rev. If you hadn't come to me and gotten me thinking, I might've kept going and ended up in prison."

"What about any loose ends of your own?" Rev asked quietly.

"Vaca was it, and I gave him the cash he needed to replace all that gear. It's now on the bottom of the bay somewhere, and he's probably still over at Boat Depot picking out all brand-new electronics. Trust me, he won't say a word."

Rev nodded, "He's a good man."

"Yeah, which is why I wanted to help him in the first place. But like they say, no good deed goes unpunished."

"You know Sean, if you had given him cash in the first place, you wouldn't be out of that business now. That would've been the real punishment, especially if you'd have ended up getting caught. So maybe you're looking at this from the wrong perspective. Maybe you got a cheap lesson by dodging a bullet."

It was the second time in a week that Rev had called him by his given name, so Rut thought hard about what he'd said. He nodded, "You know, you have a great way of getting folks to look at things from both sides, Rev."

"That's the idea, Rut. There are always two sides to every story, and usually the truth is somewhere in the middle."

"I owe you a lot."

"Buy me lunch, and we'll call it even."

"WHAT'S the matter with you this afternoon?" Angel noticed Cammie had been quiet and preoccupied ever since she came back with the limes. The lunch rush was now over, and this was the first time they'd had a chance to talk.

"Rut was next door and never even stopped by to say hello."

Angel was taken aback since she was certain there was a mutual attraction between the two, not just one-sided. Walking away and ignoring Cammie wasn't like Rut at all. "Did you end up over at his place the other night?"

"What? No! I mean yes, but only long enough for him to put on dry clothes."

Word had gotten out about what had happened to Dawn. "So, did you get a look at his... equipment?" Angel asked, with a smirk and a raised eyebrow.

"No! I was in the other room. Sheesh, only you would ask me something like that."

"Not only would I ask about that, but I'd have done it, too. Like I told you, that view is pretty spectac..."

"Stop! I don't want to hear any more about what you saw, or what you two did, okay? Just leave it alone, will you?"

"Uh-oh. The teaser doesn't like being teased. Sounds to me like somebody has a case of Rut, even before seeing him naked."

"Angel, please, just drop it."

"Looks like he won't." She nodded in the direction of the entrance, where Rut had just walked in, smiling broadly.

"Two of my favorite ladies! How are y'all today?"

Angel glanced at Cam, "Much better now, I'd say. Are you here for lunch, Rut?"

He gave Cam a curious look and replied, "Just ate next door. Had to meet up with a couple of people, and thought I'd stop by and say hi since I was around."

Cam looked relieved. "I'm glad you did. I had to pop over next door for a sec, and I saw you were with that customer again, so I left you two alone."

"Ex-customer. Then I had a long lunch with Rev. You didn't think I'd leave without saying hello, did you?"

Angel said, "Of course she didn't! We all know that's not your style." She gave Cam an "I told you so" glance and smile.

"Are we still on for dinner tomorrow night?" Cam asked.

"Looking forward to it. Hey, I need to get back to the 'yard. Call you later after work?"

"Sure." She smiled as he turned and left.

"You two have dinner plans tomorrow night and you were all worried? Make that you have a *severe* case of Rut. Where's he taking you?"

"*Rooftops* at *Bayside*. I've never been there, and I hear it's fantastic."

"Yeah, it is, and unbelievably expensive. Sounds like a 'seal the deal' dinner to me. Never even took me there, I guess I should've held out on him like you." Angel winked.

"No! It's just dinner out, that's all."

"Uh-huh. You know it's funny being on the outside looking in, knowing the two of you better than you know yourselves."

"I thought you said he didn't rush you," Cam replied.

"He didn't. I was the one who rushed him. You know, kinda like you're probably about to do after such a big night out."

∽

"THIS PLACE IS BEAUTIFUL, and what a great view!" Cam exclaimed.

She and Rut had arrived just in time to watch a spectacular Chesapeake Bay sunset. *Rooftops* was the open-air grill above *Bayside Resort and Marina's* main restaurant on one end of the hotel. It looked out over the marina to the south, and the beach and bay to the west. Over in the corner, a chef manned the open pit charcoal grill, cooking house-aged prime meats to perfection. Either the food or the view would be enough of a draw by itself, but combined they became the reason it was such an award-winning destination.

Rut said, "Casey and Dawn bought and renovated this place a few years ago when they moved up from Florida. The hotel had been shuttered for years, and the marina was a smuggler's haven."

"Wow! You'd never know it, looking at the place now."

They'd just ordered drinks when Casey and Dawn walked in along with another couple. Dawn spotted them and led her party over. Rut and Cam stood up, and she hugged them both. Casey shook hands with Rut and kissed Cam on her cheek.

"We've got to stop meeting like this, or people are going to talk," Dawn joked. "I want you guys to meet our friends and partners, Eric Clarke, and his better half, Candi Ryan. Rut Rutledge and Cammie Pinder."

"I heard how you two rescued Dawn. She was so lucky you came along when you did," Candi said.

"We all are," Eric added, shaking Rut's hand.

"Rut was the one who went in after her. All I did was help pull her up on the dock. She was already coming around by then," Cam said.

Casey shook his head, "It was a team effort, and Cammie was attending to her when I got to them. I only wish we'd caught the guy so I could've bounced him around some myself."

Casey was six feet tall, and while he was no gym rat, he was very fit and trim. Rut had no doubt that he'd have gone after Dawn's attacker since he'd been in several scrapes of his own, including one where he shot a murderous strip club owner. One thing Casey didn't lack was courage.

Dawn said, "Well, I wanted to say hello. Don't forget to let me know what night is good for you two for dinner. In fact, let's pick one now. How about this Thursday?"

Cam nodded, and Rut said, "That'd be great, thanks."

Dawn beamed. "Perfect. Cocktails at six-thirty. We'll see you at the boat."

After the foursome moved across the room to their table, Cam said, "Those two looked familiar."

"They should. She's an ex-congresswoman, and he's a well-known billionaire businessman who's in with the Shaws on this place as well as several others."

"How do you know all this?"

He shrugged, "The ESVA Telegraph, both the paper and the word-of-mouth one. Nice to know who the players are around town. Never know when it might come in handy."

"And now they all know your name."

"Both our names."

# 7

## NEW FRIENDS

"That was the best meal I've had since I can't remember when," Cam said.

"I felt the same way about the other night's pizza, but that was probably because of the company," Rut replied.

Cam smiled, "That may be the biggest part of what made tonight's dinner so special too."

Eric Clarke walked up to their table. "Rut, Cammie, the four of us are going to go have a nightcap on my boat, and I wondered if you two would like to join us."

Rut glanced at Cammie, and she nodded enthusiastically. "Sure, thanks. Let me just pay the bill, and we can meet you there. Which one is it?"

"It's the *Miss E*, but Casey already paid your bill and left the tip. So if you're ready, come on and walk over with us."

The three couples strolled slowly around the marina basin and through a locked gate in the security fence on the far side. Cam had tucked her arm through Rut's as they made their way around. It was a beautiful and still summer night, and the dark water of the marina was like a sheet of glass. Lights from the docks and several of the boats reflected across the surface. They walked down a long floating dock that ran parallel to the edge of the basin, passing a half dozen large yachts. They finally stopped at the gangway of a seventy-five-foot vintage Trumpy yacht. Candi led the way up onto the side deck and back to the stern. Rut took in all the details of the yacht along the route, noting that it was in perfect condition. That was something which didn't come cheap with a classic wooden yacht such as this one.

Though there weren't any of the crew in sight, the bar on the covered aft deck had been fully and recently stocked with fruit garnishes, and the ice bucket was filled with fresh ice. Eric bartended, then settled onto one of the cushioned rattan loveseats with Candi after everyone got a drink. He raised his glass, "To our two new friends who saved the life of our dear friend."

Cam looked over at Rut, both of them were hesitant to raise their glasses in a toast to themselves. Then he shrugged and raised his as she followed suit. After everyone had a sip, Rut said, "We just happened to be in the right place at the right time. I'm just glad the band didn't do another encore."

"Not half as glad as me!" Dawn quipped, and the group chuckled.

Eager to change the subject, Cam said, "Your boat is beautiful. I think this is the most varnish I've ever seen in one place. It takes real talent to lay it down that smooth on a vertical surface." She motioned to the cabin bulkhead, which looked like brown-colored glass.

"Thanks! You really know your boat maintenance. Does that come from having a boyfriend with a boatyard?"

For a second, she thought about correcting him about Rut being her "boyfriend," but she didn't want to seem rude. "No, more from my late father owning an outboard, and spending a lot of time on it as a kid. I've been around marinas enough to appreciate good boats and great workmanship."

Rut spoke up, "We don't get a lot of boats with varnish in our 'yard. We specialize more in workboats than yachts. Very few with teak and varnish, mostly just gelcoat and paint. It was that way when I bought the place over ten years ago, and we've tried living up to its reputation with the local watermen. Even if we kept our prices the same, if we were to start hauling yachts, they'd get it in their heads that we're too expensive. I like helping those guys, the ones who still make a living by working on the water. There are fewer of them every year, though we're lucky enough to keep a steady and loyal clientele. And that loyalty runs both ways. There's a 'yard that's more attuned to yachts and sportfish boats a couple of miles over from me, *Albury's Boat Works*. They do great finish work."

"Carlton Albury is a friend of ours," Dawn said.

Rut nodded, "Mine too."

Eric was now sitting back quietly, observing Rut and Cammie. Rut noticed this and assumed it was something he normally did around new people. Candi told him, "Oh, don't mind Eric. He still has a phobia of being in groups of more than three people, especially new people."

"Casey too," Dawn said. "You should've seen the two of them when they first met, completely paranoid about each other. Fortunately, they got over it quickly and became friends."

"Speaking of that, I'm glad you don't feel awkward having drinks with one of your employees," Cammie blurted out. She'd been feeling self-conscious around Dawn and Casey, and was glad to have brought that out in the open.

Dawn was taken aback, not realizing that she'd felt this way. She paused a beat to think before answering, not wanting to make things worse. "First, I don't do things that make me feel awkward, Cammie. You're someone who showed her inner character the other night, and that's who we invited to dinner as well as drinks, not an employee. And for the record, you aren't technically our employee, even though Casey, Eric, and I are all investors in *Mallard Cove*. Murph and Lindsay are the majority owners there, so you really work for them." She saw that Cammie had tensed up somewhat after having raised the subject. "So relax, put that out of your mind, and be yourself. I try not to go places where I can't do all three of those things." She smiled at Cam, who then nodded in agreement.

Now mostly reassured, the real Cammie did come out, and her personality was quickly winning over the other two couples like it had with Rut. Eric continued watching and listening, almost until it was time to go, then he addressed Cammie. "Here's the thing, Cammie. If I only socialized with the other people on the Forbes list, I'd be miserable. I don't even want to sit and have a drink with half of 'em. I judge people by who they are, not what they're worth or who they work for. From what I've seen tonight, and from what I've heard from Dawn and Casey, I think they've made a good choice by having you two as friends. I don't know if you've heard yet that we're building a new Jarrett Bay sportfisherman together. And I don't know if y'all fish, but I hope you'll end up doing some fishing with us when it's done, and that we see you two around *C2* a bit."

DAWN TOOK Cam by the arm as they walked to the parking lot. "You sure impressed the hell out of Eric tonight."

That caught her completely off-guard. "How?"

"By being upfront and honest that you felt kind of awkward. Like Candi said, he can feel the same way at times. But he has a hard time expressing himself around new people. I think he admires you for having done that, and it helped make him feel more relaxed and comfortable with you guys."

"He. Admires me. Are you serious?"

Dawn laughed. "I know Eric, and yes, I'm serious. You and Rut are an impressive couple."

"Uh, about that Dawn, we aren't really 'a couple.' We've only gone out a handful of times."

"Could've fooled me. Actually, you did. Probably the rest of us too. He must think a lot of you to take you to *Rooftops*."

Anxious to get away from this subject, Cam said, "By the way, thank you and Casey for picking up our tab tonight, you didn't need to do that."

Dawn rolled her eyes, "Oh, puleeze, it was the least we could do. I hope you enjoyed your meal."

"Absolutely." She paused, "Um, Eric said he hoped that he would see us around '*C2*' a bit. Do you know what he was talking about?"

"I do. And you'll find out on Thursday. Be sure to bring along your bathing suits, it's going to be a very casual evening."

Cam could see Dawn wasn't about to be more forthcoming, so she didn't push the issue. Then they reached their cars, and the couples said goodnight.

Once in Rut's truck she told him, "Well that was interesting."

"Yeah. Not something that happens every day, for sure."

"Dawn said she thought we were an impressive couple." She instantly regretted having said it, and mentally kicked herself. She didn't want him to think she was trying to push him into a relationship.

"Casey said pretty much the same thing." He didn't start the truck since she seemed to want to talk, and he wanted to encourage her.

Cam said, "I don't know what surprised me more, that they thought we were impressive, or that we were a couple. Not that you aren't impressive, I was talking more about me, and the fact that they think we're a couple, even though we've only been out on a couple of dates..."

"You're babbling, Cam. Enough about who is or isn't impressive."

She stopped. "I guess I am. I babble when I get nervous."

"You were nervous back there with them, but you got over it pretty fast. So why would you be nervous now with me?"

"Because I've just been on a date that was one of the best, ever. Because together we impressed people tonight, people that other people think are impressive. That doesn't happen a lot, at least to me. And because Angel said this is a 'seal the deal' date, and I should push to go home with you tonight, and I'm nervous about that. And I just said impressive again." She sighed.

"Cam, just because other people admire them doesn't mean that you need to."

"You don't think the Shaws, Candi, and Eric are impressive people?" She mentally kicked herself for using that word again.

"Actually, yeah, I do. But not because other people do. I make up my own mind about both things and people. And like I said, you should too." He paused. "By the way, Angel is a friend, but I don't run my life, and especially not my love life, according to what she says. She has her own set of rules that she plays by. I didn't and don't buy into them. Which is probably part of why we didn't last that long as lovers. When you think about it, it's funny that we've stayed friends. She has her own set schedule about... things. Me? I just do what I feel is right at the time, and I don't give in to outside pressures. Frankly, I wish you had thought of it as such a great date before the part about having run into the Shaws and their friends."

"How do you know I didn't?"

"Because ever since we got back into this truck, there have been five other people in here with us: those two couples and Angel. I was hoping for just the two of us. That's how I'd have known that we were on the right track, that it had been a great date for both of us... because of us." He sighed. "But Angel was wrong. This wasn't a 'seal the deal' dinner, it was a 'thank you' dinner for something you did but didn't even realize you'd done. Since the night is apparently now blown to hell, I need to tell you how big a mistake you almost made.

"Up until a few days ago, I was a reseller of stolen electronics and fishing gear. I could rationalize it by telling you how originally I was only going to dig myself out of the financial hole my divorce created, and without doing it I could have never gotten out from under a loan shark, but I'd be kidding both of us. I did it because it was easy money, and that's why I kept doing it after I paid him back. But then I started feeling guilty, and the other day when you said that marina thieves were the lowest scum of the earth, it hit me right between the eyes. It was the final reinforcement I needed to hear to bring me back to my senses. So I got out of the business partly because I knew I'd never be able to look you in the eye if I didn't. Or look be able to keep looking at myself in the mirror. Thank you for that. But I'm sorry I'm not the guy you thought I was."

"That's what you were arguing about with that guy at the *Catamaran*."

"Please forget you ever saw him, or me with him."

There was silence in the truck for a minute then Cam said, "Please take me home. My home. And just drop me at the curb."

Rut started the motor. "I'm sorry, Cam. And for the record, I do think you're very impressive, but not because anyone else does."

~

THE NEXT AFTERNOON Rut was on his hands and knees sanding the cockpit deck of the *Scarab* and had worked his way up under the lean seat. He'd wanted to do something mindless after what had been such a miserable day. He'd been rerunning his talk with Cam over and over in his head, mentally kicking himself. It wasn't until that point that he began to realize how much he already liked her.

"I want you to tell me all of it, especially the 'why' part," Cam said. She'd climbed the ladder again and was now peeking over the gunwale. She startled Rut, who raised up and banged his head on the bottom of the aluminum frame on the seat.

"Ow! You scared the crap outta me!"

"Good, I hope your head hurts. What, did you think one of your old business partners had shown up and was going to shoot you? If I was gonna do that, I'd have done it twenty hours ago when you ruined one of the best nights of my life. So, spill. Please explain to me why I couldn't sleep last night, and why I ripped Angel's head off today for no apparent reason. Tell me why I should think that somehow you are still a decent person who just made a dumbass mistake. Explain to me why I'm not an idiot for not having written you off as damaged goods that are completely beyond repair, and why I'm not even more of an idiot for showing up here now. In other words, convince me that you have some shred of redeeming value and that I'm not crazy for thinking, feeling, or wanting to believe that it exists somewhere deep down in you. Because I really don't know why I so desperately want to believe that's true. So, either do that or send me on my way."

"Can we go over and sit on my porch? This isn't going to be a two-minute conversation."

"Do you still have a couple of my beers left?"

"Yes."

"Then okay."

An hour later he was completely spent. He'd told Cam things about the divorce and his life before and after it that he'd never told anyone. He even included things he'd never before been willing to admit to himself. He didn't want to tell her all the details about becoming a fence, but they all came spilling out anyway. He wasn't sure if it was because the time had come to confide in someone, or because Eric had been right and she was someone worthy of his trust. Or maybe because he realized he had started to feel a real connection with her, at least until he blew it all to hell the night before. He wanted it back, whatever it was, if it could be gotten back. He couldn't tell by looking at her face.

She sat in silence for a few minutes, digesting what he'd said. "That's everything, and it's all true?" she asked.

"Everything. You deserved nothing less than the truth. I won't lie to you."

"Did you call Dawn or Casey and cancel tomorrow night?"

"No. I figured you might've."

"I probably should have, but I didn't."

He winced.

"And since I didn't, you can pick me up at six."

"Maybe we should postpone it until we're on a friendlier basis again."

She replied, "Or not. Now we're gonna pick up a pizza and more beer and talk right here on this porch tonight until there isn't anything left to talk about. If that doesn't get us back to a comfortable level of friendly, then we'll cancel. And not just dinner."

"I've already told you everything, Cam."

"Not you. Me. I'm going to tell you why I'm here on ESVA, and a lot more about me that you don't know. There are some big reasons why I came back here today. You deserve to know all about those, too. Just as I deserved to know about what you had been doing. You showed me yours, and now it's my turn to show you mine."

# 8

# INSIDE SCOOP

*Virginia Beach, the next morning...*

MANGO WAS on his way to his "office," which was really a corner booth in one of the delicatessens he owned. The prior owner now managed this one for him; a tradeoff for keeping his knees intact after getting way behind on his payments. Turning over this deli property and his other one down in Hatteras, NC, had only covered the principal, not the back interest. As Mango walked down the sidewalk he spotted a lone bike lock, left behind without a bike on a rack in front of the library. It was a signal that was put there for him, and he knew it would disappear by this evening. As he approached his deli, he beckoned to one of the neighborhood kids on the sidewalk and explained what he needed. Twenty minutes later the kid came in the back door of the deli, making his way to Mango's booth where he exchanged an envelope for twenty bucks in cash. He swore he had been careful not to be followed. The tape that had held it underneath a newspaper rack two blocks away was still hanging from the envelope.

Mango opened it and read the letter it contained. *"You are headed for trouble. GJ referral first week of next month. No way for me to derail it."* The money he paid that mole in the Attorney General's office was proving to have been worth it. But a federal grand jury referral was his worst nightmare. If the AG got a "true bill" it would mean an indictment, and an open season on him by the feds. He'd have no choice but to run and disappear. Mango's brow was still furrowed when Frankie Hicks slid into the booth across from him.

"Trouble?" he asked.

"Yeah, but I think I have a way around it. Know the redhead your moron Joey threw off the dock the other night? I need ta know everything about her. This much I already know, she's either married or engaged, and she lives on a boat over at *Mallard Cove* and owns part of the place. Find out who the guy is that's doin' her, and exactly where they live. I need ta know all about that guy too, right down ta his jock size and what time he takes a whiz in the morning, got it?"

"Uh-huh. I'm guessin' you don't want Joey on this one, right?"

"What tipped ya off about that? The fact I'm not tellin' him ta do this, or because she'd spot him a mile away? I don't want that numbskull within ten miles of *Mallard Cove*, you understand? And make sure there's no connection back ta me whatsoever if ya get caught."

"Got it. Me an' Mikey will dig into it, and we won't get caught."

"Do it pronto, we don't have much time."

∽

RUT WOKE up after only getting a few short hours of sleep. Sunlight had just started backlighting the blinds on his bedroom windows. He felt Cammie stir beside him, and he rolled onto his side to look at her. She must've felt the movement, and her eyes opened then focused on his. At first, he thought he saw a glimmer of happiness in them, but it was quickly replaced by uncertainty. A LOT of uncertainty.

Rut said, "Good morning, sunshine."

"Good morning yourself," Cam replied.

"Not a morning person, are we?"

"Maybe when I get more than an hour or so of shuteye."

"That was one long conversation we had."

She snorted, "You know darn well it wasn't just the conversation that kept me up so late and tired me out."

"You didn't seem so grumpy last night. And it's funny, I haven't thought of pizza and beer as a 'seal the deal' dinner since I was in high school." He tried lightening the mood and grinned at first, but then his smile faded when it wasn't returned. "I'm sorry if you've got a case of buyer's remorse."

"It's not about what you think. The only other guy who knows some of what I told you ended up divorcing me over it after I finally told him. At least it was part of the reason. So I don't know why I felt the need to reciprocate by giving you something that you can now hold over my head."

He reached across and put his palm on her cheek. "That's not who I am, Cam, I'd never do that. I hope you'll give me the chance to prove that to you."

An impish grin slowly crept onto her face. In an attempt to deflect the question, she said, "Have I ever denied you anything?"

"Funny lady. But I'm serious. It's not something you need to worry about. It stays with me. All of it."

She sighed heavily and looked serious again. "It's not like I have a choice now. It felt so good to share all that last night, and then be... close to you. But now this morning I feel I've got a ton of weight on my shoulders, and it's like I've put some of that weight on you now, too."

"Right back at you. There is something about you that made me not hold anything back. Then I felt stupid for having told you everything and maybe messing up a good friendship or whatever this is. I'm glad it didn't end right then and there."

"That's where I am this morning, Rut. Feeling really dumb."

"Which is the last thing you are, and you sure shouldn't feel like that." He pulled the sheet down and with his finger he traced the four-inch hook-shaped scar that ran from her nipple down along under the bottom of her left breast. "This wasn't your fault. None of it was."

She shuddered and looked away from him. "I know. The bastard told me it was his mark, and that it meant I'd be his forever. It looked a lot bigger back then when I was only twelve." She looked back at him. "It was the smallest but the most visible of all the marks he left on me, Rut. My parents knew it all after a while, but now they're gone. And like I said, my ex knew a lot of it, but I never could bring myself to tell him why I couldn't have kids, or what exactly happened to my rapist; he didn't want to know any of the details. You're now the only one left in this world who knows everything. I'm sorry to have burdened you with it, but I needed to share it with someone."

"I'm glad you did, and it's going to stay with me." He put his arms around her and pulled her to him. He felt how tense she was at first, then felt the tension start to flow out of her as he silently stroked her hair. "I'm telling you that you've got the scar all wrong. It isn't that bastard's mark, it's your survivor badge. Take ownership of it by seeing what he said for the lie that it is. Then you'll take back all the power from him he believed he'd taken from you. Look at it as a reminder of how strong you can be when you need to. He's gone, and you're still here. You beat him and got past it, past him. You've not only survived but thrived. Eric was wrong, you aren't impressive, you're way beyond that, you're frigging amazing."

A few minutes later, in a quiet voice she said, "I don't know why I put all that on you, especially so soon, but now I am feeling better about it. There's something about you and how you look at things so differently, like the scar. Is it crazy to think I sensed that in you? All these years it has been something I hid because I was ashamed of it, instead of realizing it could remind me that I really can get through anything."

"Didn't your therapist tell you the same thing?"

"I've never been to a therapist, I worked through it all myself. It was tough enough telling my parents. They thought if the story got out I'd go to jail, so they told me to never talk about it. Either they believed that, or they were ashamed. In any case, I kept it to myself."

Rut was stunned that she'd never been through therapy after such a traumatic event, and amazed that she'd come through it seemingly as well as she had.

"When you told me what you had done, Rut, that shook me. I'd have never pegged you as a criminal. But hearing how I helped push you out of it, even in a small way, I'm glad I did. It made me feel worthwhile. Made me think maybe we could help each other."

Rut winced when she called him a criminal.

She paused, then continued. "You not only look at things differently, you make others do it too. You're showing me that people can screw up and still find their way back to being good folks, especially when they have help getting there. I realized then what I needed, someone who would listen and try to understand."

"No, you don't need anybody like that. You've already got me."

She snuggled against him, thinking back about what everything the two of them had said to each other over the past dozen hours. Finally, she moved until she was face to face with him. "My shift doesn't start until eleven." She raised an eyebrow questioningly.

"The 'yard opens in an hour and a half."

She smiled, "If that's all the time we have right now, then let's not waste it."

BEFORE HE WENT TO WORK, Rut told her to make herself at home, that she was welcome to hang out, shower, and fix herself breakfast if she wanted. She put on a long tee shirt of his, made coffee, and wandered around the house to maybe understand him better. No pictures with his ex anywhere, and that was good, but there were no family pictures either. This was another thing they had in common. She wondered how much of the furniture his ex had taken in the divorce, because most of what was here seemed relatively new, and the style reflected him. Tasteful, rugged, but simple. In fact, there didn't seem to be any evidence of a woman's touch anywhere in the house, not even Angel's. She hated to admit it to herself, but that part really pleased her. He wasn't hanging on to mementos of old flames.

She wasn't sure where this was headed, where *they* were headed, but she was relatively certain she didn't need to worry there might be someone else in the wings. He had her fooled at first, thinking he was a total "boy scout." But he hadn't really lied, it was more like an error of omission, she thought. And after last night, what else could there be? She told him how her rapist had infected her with the STD that had attacked her ovaries, destroying them as they had been about to mature enough to start producing eggs. How she'd hidden from her parents and everyone else the fact that she'd been attacked. She hadn't known about STDs and the damage they could cause, and how easily gonorrhea could be cured before causing any damage, especially if it was treated quickly. Cammie told him how it had been her fault that she could never bear children because she'd kept silent, instead of going to the doctor before the damage was done.

But out on his dark porch in the wee hours of the morning, he gave her his own brand of absolution. He told her to quit blaming herself, and got her to look at it from the outside in. Would she now blame some other twelve-year-old girl who had been raped and scarred, completely petrified, believing that she'd be going to jail because she had retaliated against her attacker in his sleep? No, he told her, no sane person would, no matter how that happened. Because of her courage, she'd made certain he would never do that again to any other young girl.

She had told him how she managed to free herself from the ropes he'd used to tie her to the bed where he lay sleeping next to her. But what she did next was what made her keep silent about the ordeal. Her eyes were accustomed to the low light of the room and she went around to his side of the bed, retrieving the knife from his bedside table. The same one he'd used to cut her breast. Then she plunged it into the left side of his chest, and into his lung. He woke up screaming, the sound lessening as the air escaped through the hole as the lung collapsed. She took advantage of his pain and confusion to stab him in the other side, piercing that lung as well. Now unable to get all but short gasps of air as both lungs collapsed, his strength quickly faded as the oxygen in his bloodstream was depleted. He lashed out, trying to grab her in the dim light of the room, but she stayed just out of his reach until he lay there quietly gasping, making a gurgling sound as the blood seeped into his lungs.

At this point, EMTs might have still been able to save his life had she run and called for help. Instead, she used that same knife to sever his genitals, placing them on his chest between the stab wounds. She wasn't sure if it was the blood loss from his crotch, or the asphyxiation from the collapsed lungs that finished him. Frankly, she didn't care. Cammie knew though that she'd now crossed a big legal line that would prevent her from being able to tell anyone what happened. She went into the bathroom and washed off all the blood. She found a first aid kit and bandaged the wound on her chest, applying butterfly bandages. Having seen enough crime shows on television, she knew she now had to destroy any evidence that could lead authorities back to her. She found all her clothes and got dressed, making sure not to leave anything behind.

Fortunately, her rapist had an older gas stove, the kind you had to light with matches. Cammie opened one burner valve, knowing it would eventually fill the house with gas, yet one burner being left on wouldn't be that suspicious. Walking back into the bedroom she spotted a kerosene lamp. In those days, power outages in Crozet during storms were a frequent event, and most folks kept an alternate light source. Cammie lit the lantern and placed it high up on a dresser, then went out the front door and walked the two blocks to her home in the dark, never once looking back. She climbed back in her bedroom window, the same one he'd come through while she had been sleeping. The explosion happened twenty minutes later as she lay in bed, and it shook her house. It was only after that she was able to finally close her eyes and go to sleep.

AFTER SHE SHOWERED, Cammie put Rut's tee shirt in his laundry hamper and got dressed in the clothes she'd worn last night. As she left the house she spotted an old bearded guy on the dock, climbing out of a purple-bottomed skiff, and now headed for where she was parked. It turned out his car was next to hers.

"'Mornin' there, young lady."

Cammie laughed, "I haven't been called a young lady in quite a while."

"Well, you're a lot younger'n me. I'm Daniels. Friend of Rut's are ya?"

She nodded. "New friend. Cammie."

"Then you should know, you won't find a finer friend than Rut, Cammie. Does an awful lot for us watermen an' our families, ya know. Anyway, you have yourself a nice day."

"You too." She climbed into her car, happy to escape the cloud of stale body odor that had drifted her way. But she was also glad to have heard what Daniels said about Rut and the local watermen's families. It fit what she hoped and believed to be the truth about him. The real truth, the one he was working his way back to.

## 9

# ONE BADASS

To say that Rut had been preoccupied most of the day would've been a gross understatement. If someone had told him yesterday that as a twelve-year-old, Cammie had killed her rapist, sliced and diced him, then blown up his house to destroy the evidence, he'd have thought they were nuts. Especially since she hadn't seen a professional therapist, and all the people in her life who knew her secrets had either passed away or pushed her away after they found out. They'd left her to deal with it by herself. The fact that she'd held it together all alone through the years was a testament to her hidden and mostly silent strength.

Now Rut admired her for it. Sitting on his porch in the dark last night, at first her story was, to say the least, alarming. He hadn't known whether to believe her or not at the time. But as the pain continued spilling out of her, he'd realized this wasn't a story someone could've spontaneously made up; the pain he was hearing was too real. Though later in the dim light of his bedroom when he saw that scar for the first time, it was somehow strangely reassuring. You couldn't fake the apprehensive look on her face, and he realized this was a pivotal moment for the two of them. As she searched his face for a reaction, he knew if he had even slightly hinted at revulsion to it or how she'd gotten it, Cam would've been gone from his life. He'd have added another invisible scar on top of that visible one. She wasn't just searching for a reaction but hoping for an ally. She was tired of wandering through this emotional desert all by herself, and her telling him all the details was a brave first step.

That's when he realized that for whatever reason the stars had aligned to send her to him for help, and for her to help him as well. He silently accepted his part of the challenge and the responsibility, and was now determined to help her change the way she viewed things. He let her know he accepted and even approved of what she'd done to the man who'd stolen her from her own bed, robbed her of her innocence and much of her childhood. The bastard had gotten what was coming to him. Rut said he was not only good with it, but hoped he'd have had the courage to do it himself. He had no doubt her rapist planned on eventually killing her; she'd seen his face, and knew where he lived. Right then, in the dim light on his porch, he saw something on Cam's face that he first mistook for relief. Then he realized it was much more; it was an acceptance of him not just as a friend she was starting to date, but the truly worthy confidant she needed and had been searching for. In just a week, she'd discovered in him something she hadn't found in all the years she'd spent with her husband; complete trust. Her ex didn't want to hear about any of it, wanting to deny it ever happened. He acted as if he was the one it had all happened to. When she finally left Crozet, it was even more about leaving him behind rather than what had happened there two and a half decades ago.

∼

"Well, someone looks like she's in a much better mood today. Get lucky last night?" Angel asked.

"I'm sorry I was such a bitch to you yesterday."

"You didn't answer my question." Her interest was now piqued.

"No, I ignored your question. There's a big difference." Cammie gave her a sideways glance, hoping this would end the inquisition, even though she knew better.

"Oh, so you *did* get laid! Good for you. Wait... we *are* still talking about Rut, right?"

"You may be. But I'm not talking, period."

"C'mon, Cam, I deserve details! After all, I was the one who set you two up."

"You what? How do you figure that one?"

Angel grinned, "Because I gave you all the details about when he and I were together. About how the morning view was so stunn..."

"Hold it! I never asked. And if you'll recall, I tried to get you to stop being so graphic. So now, if we're going to remain friends, there will be new ground rules. No more talk about your past with Rut, and that means *everything* about your past with him. It would just invite comparisons, which wouldn't be fair to you." Cam did another sideways glance, this one with a wide grin.

"Wouldn't be... whaaaat?" Angel put on her best Terri Clark voice and belted out, "Girls lie too, we don't care how much money you make, or what you drive or what you weigh. And size don't matter, anyway. Girls lie toooo..."

Cam sang back, "He's easy on the eyessss, and good on the heart..."

"Hey! That's not how it goes! If you're gonna sing Terri Clark, you can't screw with the lyrics."

Cammie smiled to herself. She knew changing the words to one of Angel's favorite performer's songs would distract her and derail the conversation. Fortunately for her, their first customers of the day chose to walk in then, and the rest of their shift stayed busy.

As they walked out together after their shift, Angel asked, "So, are you seeing Rut again tonight?"

"Maybe."

"You are really going to play hardass on this, aren't you?"

"I told you, there are new ground rules."

Angel fumed, "You said those were about my past with Rut, not your 'here and now' with him. You still have to share details."

"Not really."

"At least tell me where you're going."

Cammie tried hiding a smile. "Who says we're going anywhere? Maybe we're staying in."

"No, no, no, make him take you somewhere first. If you don't make him take you out, he'll get used to sex, sex, sex all the time and then you'll never get him to take you anywhere."

"Okay, I'll tell you one detail about last night if you'll shut up."

"Deal. What happened?"

"We sat out on his porch and talked until one a.m."

"What? No sex?"

"Sorry. You're limited to one detail." Cammie smiled at Angel as she climbed into her car, leaving her friend fuming and wondering in the parking lot as she drove off.

∼

CAMMIE WAS glad when Rut texted her to come over to his place, saying he had something he wanted to show her and then they could leave from there. She didn't know what the surprise was, but she had her own ulterior motive. Now it meant they'd have to come back to his place after dinner so she could retrieve her car, but she hoped she wouldn't be driving home until tomorrow morning. She wondered if he hadn't had the same thought.

As she pulled up, she saw him standing next to the *Scarab*. He came over to her car and greeted her with a kiss. "Hey there."

"Hey yourself. You smell like paint."

He grinned. "Surprise! Come see what I did this afternoon." He led her over to the boat and motioned for her to go up the ladder. "Don't get in, the deck's still wet. But tomorrow is gonna be splash day."

She climbed up two rungs then looked over the gunwale at the interior. "It came out beautiful, Rut! I wish I could be here to see her go in, but I've got first shift again tomorrow, and don't get off until five."

"Did I mention that I own the travel lift? We can splash it whenever we want, and I'm not doing that without you being here for it." He wrapped his arms around her legs and lifted her off the stepladder, slowly lowering her to the ground as she laughed.

"I like the way you say 'we' when you talk about doing stuff."

"Yeah, and I like the way you appreciate the work I put into her, and how she came out."

Cam cocked her head and pursed her lips slightly before saying, "You *are* still talking about the boat, right?"

For the first time since their after-dinner talk at *Rooftops*, Rut saw some sparkle in her eyes. "Of course! The *Scarab* is finished, but you're still a work in progress."

"Takes one to know one. Go get a shower so we can go. You reek."

"It's boatyard cologne, real expensive stuff. Eau de polyurethane." He laughed as she scowled. "But okay, for you, I'll shower. You know there's room for two in there, right?"

"I also know we need to leave in ten minutes or we'll be late. So go! And don't forget they said to bring a bathing suit." She smiled, now certain that her car would be there overnight.

AT THE FENCE Rut punched in the code Dawn had texted Cammie, and the gate rolled open. Once past the woods they got their first daylight view of the private marina.

Cam said, "Wow, this place is much bigger than it looked in the dark." Ahead were a handful of slips that contained various boats and a couple of custom house barges. All the slips had covered parking behind them. Over to the left was a large enclosed boathouse, and on the far right against the bulkhead was *Lady Dawn*, which looked much larger and even more spectacular than she had the night they brought Dawn home. They parked next to her gangway and made their way aboard, knocking on the side of the salon. Dawn opened the side door, hugging each of them as they went inside.

"I'm so glad you guys could make it! I hope you don't mind, we're eating over at *C2* instead of here. And it's only burgers, but the ones Casey grills are killer!"

Cam said, "Burgers would be swell. And Eric mentioned *C2* the other night too. What is that?"

"Oh, sorry, I forgot you guys haven't been here before except to drop me off. To make a short story long, Casey and I decided to move out of *Bayside* after we lost a lot of our privacy there. But that part's a story for another day. Anyway, we moved the boats to *Mallard Cove*, and one day when he was wandering around the woods he stumbled onto this little harbor. The inlet had an old sunken wood freighter blocking the view of it from the channel, so we'd never realized what was here when we passed by on the water. The boathouse was crumbling, and the property was all overgrown. We bought it, added the docks, fixed the boathouse, and built *C2*. Sandy Morgan named the marina *Casey's Cove*, and *C2* stands for the *Cove Club*. I could tell you about it, but I'm going to let you see for yourself. It started because Casey lost his pool table to his first wife back in Florida. I'll let him tell you the rest."

Rut said, "Oh, I didn't realize you were Casey's second wife."

Cammie poked him and Dawn laughed. "It's okay, Cam. No, technically I'm his third wife, but I prefer to say that I'm his last one."

"Were you talking about Sandy Morgan the writer? He comes in the *Beach Bar* sometimes with Captain Bill Cooper." Cam was anxious to get off the subject of "exes."

"Oh, you know 'Captain Baloney,' do you? He and Sandy are good friends, not that they'd admit it. And yes, I meant that Sandy. He lives on the trawler over next to the boathouse."

"Yeah, those two are a trip, always arguing over who will pay their tab. I offered to give them separate checks once, and they looked at me like I had a third eye in my head. Seems like they aren't happy unless they're arguing over beer."

Dawn laughed. "That's them. Hey, I hope you remembered your suits. I've got one over there in the changing room. And speaking of beer, would you guys like one for the walk? The sun's over the yardarm already."

They each grabbed a bottle of Red Stripe beer, then hit the dock. Dawn gave a running commentary on the boats as they strolled along. "This is *Predator*, our old *Jarrett Bay*. We're building a new one along with Eric. It's going to be named *Sharke*, a play on our two last names combined. This two-deck houseboat is *On Coastal Time*, Murph and Lindsay's home. This classic Chris Craft, *Why Knot*, belongs to Marlin and Kari Denton who are two more of our partners, as does this three-deck house barge, *Tied Knot*, which is their home. This center console Contender, *LNZ II* belongs to Murph and Lindsay. And as I said earlier this is Sandy's trawler, *Epilogue*."

Dawn opened the boathouse door and turned on the lights. The back wall held a variety of fishing gear including rods and cast nets. In the center of the room a beautiful twenty-four-foot Winter center console floated in the slip.

"Just like you like 'em, Rut. All painted decks and the only varnish being on the helm pod," Cam said.

Dawn commented, "Sounds like you and Casey have the same taste in outboards."

Rut nodded. "Looks like it. This one is beautiful, Dawn."

She nodded. "And she rides every bit as good as she looks."

Back outside, they walked past the boathouse and up a concrete walk to a covered outdoor kitchen. Casey was there in his bathing suit, lighting the charcoal in a large ceramic cooker.

"Hi, Cammie, Rut. Thanks for coming."

Rut replied, "Our pleasure, thanks for the invitation. This place is great!"

Beyond the cooking area was a large concrete deck that surrounded a combined pool and spa. A two-level, Seminole-built thatched-roof chickee stood just beyond it like a wide guard tower. A low knee wall surrounded the area, limiting sightlines from the marina basin as well as the Virginia Inside Passage waterway that ran along the eastern edge of the property. Between it and the knee wall was a concrete seaplane ramp and a helicopter pad. But the last amenity was the one that really caught Rut's eye. It looked like a house with the wall that faced the pool area made entirely of a large set of sliding glass doors.

"This place," Dawn said, "...is *C2*. The clubhouse building has guest quarters, steam room, changing rooms, bar, big screen TV, and that pool table I mentioned. We work hard, and when we play, we play just as hard."

Casey commented, "No matter how large your boat is, there's no having a pool table aboard."

Rut asked, "So you have a helicopter?" He motioned to the orange "carrot" windsock and the landing pad.

"Maybe one day, Rut. Meanwhile, Eric uses it for his. He has a pad at his office over at Fairfax in Northern Virginia, where he also lives on the top floor. I don't need to tell you how brutal the traffic can be between here and there. This way he gets to here or *Bayside* in less than a tenth of the drive time." He looked at the three of them, "Hey, why am I the only one in a bathing suit?"

"I was just going to take everyone over to change. We'll be right back," Dawn said.

Over in the clubhouse she pointed out the men's changing room for Rut, then led Cam into the women's. She started to disrobe and hang her clothes in a cubby where her bikini already waited. She was down to just panties when she saw Cammie looking at her, still in her bra and shorts, looking hesitant. Dawn could see Cam had some major tan lines, something that Dawn completely lacked.

"I forgot to tell you, a few of us work on erasing our tan lines over here, that's part of what that low wall is about. And if you'd rather wait to change until I'm done and out of here, that's fine, I'll just be a minute."

Cam shook her head, and took off her bra, bracing for any comment or question that might come over the scar. When she saw Dawn look at it with concern and not pity, she made a huge choice. "I used to have a story I made up about a horse-riding accident and a barbed-wire fence. But it wasn't true. I'm a survivor of a sexual assault that happened to me when I was twelve. Other than Rut, you're the only friend I've told the truth about it. He's convinced me that by telling the real story, this helps me finish taking the power back from the bastard who tried taking it from me."

Dawn sat down next to Cam on the changing bench, her bright blue eyes darkening with anger. "I hope the son of a bitch is still rotting in jail. And it sounds like Rut is even smarter than I thought."

For the second time in as many minutes Cam was confronted with a huge decision. She took a deep breath. She knew what she was about to say might get not just her, but Rut as well, pushed away from the Shaws. However, Rut's words kept repeating in her head, and she knew what she needed to say. "That night I made sure he'd never harm another girl again. And the cops never got called. Only you and Rut know that now."

Dawn let the enormity of what Cam both said and left unsaid sink in, then she said, "This was when you were only twelve." It was as much a statement as a question.

"Yes."

"You know, Eric Clarke was wrong about you the other night when he kept calling you impressive. You're not just impressive, you're a freakin' badass. And to let you know, you're among friends with all the residents here in *Casey's Cove*. Unfortunately, we've all had to handle things... similar things... ourselves. There's the law, and then there's justice. Sometimes the letter of the law doesn't match up with the intent, and there are simpler and more direct ways to see that justice gets served. In those cases, we've acted as our own jury.

"It's funny that I'm the one saying that since I just got picked to be on a federal grand jury. But what I'm trying to say is you're among folks who can appreciate what you had to do. You can trust all of us, and I can tell you there's not a single person here that will judge you for anything that happened back then." She smiled. "Especially since you're such a badass. And if you ever want to ditch those tan lines and get some sun on the 'girls,' you're welcome to join us on the deck when we're laying out. By the way, have you ever tried MSM on that scar? It won't totally erase it, but it'll help it fade a bit."

Cam suddenly and very forcefully reached over and hugged

Dawn, catching her off guard. Rut had been right, she was taking that power back by confronting what had happened, and it felt great. She released Dawn and said, "No, I've never tried MSM. Guess I never saw the need to since, as I guess you can tell, I don't exactly show it off very often." She smiled somewhat ruefully. "But I think I will try it, and I might even take you up on erasing a few of these tan lines, too."

"I'm glad. Now let's get changed. Casey made some of his famous smoked fish dip, and it usually goes pretty fast."

AFTER DEPLETING the dip and taking a relaxing swim, the three of them sat in chairs while Casey put five burgers in the cooker. A few minutes later a tall, dark gray and black tabby cat appeared from around the boathouse, making a beeline for the kitchen. A spry white-haired man in his seventies with a scruffy beard and a small gold hoop earring followed behind the cat. The feline froze about ten feet away when he spotted some new people, and he eyed Rut and Cammie suspiciously. Slowly he advanced toward Cam, then rubbed up against her legs as she bent down and petted him.

"Hey, he likes you, Cammie!" Sandy Morgan had spotted one of his favorite servers from the bar. "Cammie, meet KC Shaw. Not to be confused with his human namesake."

Rut leaned over to pet him just as Sandy started to say, "I wouldn't do that..."

"Ow!" KC had shredded the back of Rut's hand with his claws.

"I tried to warn you, but you didn't listen, fella," Sandy grumped. "Hey Case, you have a beer? I'm..."

"Fresh out. I know, I know. In the cooler. And hand me the little tub while you're in there."

Sandy dug into the ice, retrieving a Red Stripe and a little covered plastic box. He handed the tub to Casey as he commented, "Those burgers sure smell good. Looks like there's five of them and only four of you."

Casey said, "What, you didn't think I was already counting on you,

Sandy? I knew better since the grill smoke was headed over in your direction."

"You're a good man, Casey Shaw, in spite of what Baloney says about you being so tight with your beer."

Cam looked surprised, "Captain Cooper said something bad about Casey?"

Sandy grinned like a kid caught with his hand in the cookie jar. "Not really. But I figured if I can get him banned from the cooler, there'll be that much more for me. Plus, I like stirring up trouble for him. And please don't call him Captain Cooper, he gets such a swelled head. Around here he's either Baloney or Gilligan. The first one he tolerates, and the second one he hates, so I mostly call him by it." He turned to Rut, "And just who might you be?"

Cam said, "This is my friend, Rut Rutledge."

Rut said, "Nice to meet you. I've read a few of your books."

"Then read the rest of them, I've got a cat to feed and a boat to maintain."

Casey handed the box to Rut. "These are fresh tuna pieces. Give KC one at a time, and you'll make friends fast."

Rut looked at his bleeding hand, then down at the cat who was now fixated on the box. He took out a piece of fish and gingerly offered it to the cat in the palm of his hand. KC cautiously took it, then sat at Rut's feet while he ate it. Rut offered him another piece, which was accepted even faster. By the fourth and last piece, KC had found another new friend, an approved "fish provider."

Sandy said, "He'll recognize you from now on, but it's still not a bad idea to move slow around him for a while. Sometimes he plays with his claws out."

"That was playing?"

"No, that was a warning shot. This is playing." He took a small cat toy out of his pocket and threw it in the air as KC raced over and caught it. Then the cat tossed it back into the air, and it landed in Rut's lap. He pounced on Rut, who howled since he had landed in his lap with his claws out, finding some extra-soft tissue to puncture under his bathing suit.

"Warned you." Sandy said, as if Rut could've prevented it.

LATER, on the way back to Rut's, Cam said, "Do you think Dawn really meant it about letting us tie up and use their pool whenever we are around in your boat?"

"I don't think either one of those two ever say much they don't mean. Unlike Sandy. That man is a trip." He shook his head as he thought of several wild things Sandy had said.

Cam told Rut of her conversation with Dawn about justice, and being among like-minded people. Then she related how she'd dealt with the scar. "I think I'm going to join them some when they sunbathe over there."

"I have a set of tan sheets you might end up blending in with then. How would I be able to find you?" He winked.

"Kind of sure of yourself, aren't you? Who says I'll be in your bed again?" She tilted her head slightly as she teased him.

"Uh, I was hoping..."

She smiled, "I thought you said there was more room in the shower."

"In that case, I'll let you see for yourself."

"Okay, so long as I'm not *by* myself."

## 10

# WAVE DANCER

The next day was Angel's day off, letting her hit the beach. Of course, this didn't prevent her from hanging around the bar some, continually badgering Cammie with questions about what was going on between her and Rut. Fortunately, the long summer days meant the sun was still high in the sky when Cammie left, and Angel had gone back to laying out on the beach. Cammie made one stop at a convenience store, then drove straight over to Rut's. The *Scarab* was suspended in the straps of the travel lift in front of the haul-out slip, and Rut was giving the hull's bottom one last look before launching her.

"Hey! She looks great off the trailer."

Rut replied, "She'll look even better in the water. What's in the bag?" He motioned to a brown paper sack Cam was carrying.

She reached in the bag, removing a bottle of Jamaican Red Stripe. "I was afraid you might be going to christen her with something domestic. An island-hopping lady like this deserves nothing less than a beer from an island."

"I hadn't even thought about christening her."

"Sean Rutledge! A lady of the water as graceful as she requires a proper sendoff. I can't believe you were just going to dump her in without a ceremony."

"What, are you now taking lessons from Rev?"

"What do you mean?" she asked.

"He calls me Sean when I get in trouble and/or I disappoint him."

"Sounds like a smart fellow. But no, though I've heard of him I have yet to meet the man. And the coincidence of the whole 'Sean' thing should tell you something."

"What's that?"

"You don't want to be called 'Sean' by either of us."

Rut rolled his eyes. "Okay. You can pour beer on her bow, but no breaking the bottle. I don't want to have to sew you up, and I don't want my paint job scratched."

"Okay. So, what do we christen her as?"

"Pardon me?"

"That's a dumb name."

"I hadn't really thought about giving her a name."

"Sean Rut..."

He held up his hand. "I get it. Okay, with those twin 250-horsepower four-stroke outboards she's decently fast. How about '*Speed Demon*'?"

"Oh, I get a vote in this?"

"It was your idea so, sure."

"Then how about 'oh, hell no.' *Speed Demon*? Seriously? Are you going to start wearing a little 'weenie monokini' with tons of gold chains and a chest toupee now?"

"Okay, then you come up with a name," he said. "And you know darn well I wouldn't need a chest toupee."

"*Sand Dancer*."

"No way. Sounds like we ran aground. How about '*Wave Dancer*.' A name we came up with together."

"I like it! But since she's your boat, you should name her whatever you want."

"You want to run her some?"

"Well, sure, I'd love to."

"Then you choose; *Speed Demon* or *Wave Dancer*."

"No contest. *Wave Dancer*. If nothing else, to keep you from wearing one of those weenie thong things." She gave him a sly grin, "You'd have a hard time finding one to fit you anyway." She added a wink on top of the grin.

THEY IDLED out through the boatyard channel into Mockhorn Bay. Rut watched as Cam walked around the center console, joining him perched against the lean seat. He thought she looked hot in her boat shoes, leather anklet, short khaki shorts, *Mallard Cove* tee shirt, and aviator sunglasses. She noticed him staring. "What?"

"Nothing. Other than you look great; like you were always meant to be aboard a boat. This fits you, especially this particular boat."

"I hope you don't mean I'm old but wouldn't look bad with a fresh coat of paint."

"Hey! Don't pick on *Dancer*, she's sensitive. And no, I meant what I said, you look great. Learn how to take an honest compliment."

Cam kissed him, then leaned against his side, looping her arm through his.

Rut said, "As great as this feels, and at the risk of you stopping it, do you want to run her now?"

"Heck yes! Where are we going?"

"Dinner."

"I can't go to dinner like this! There are my work clothes."

"Yes you can, we're not going to *Rooftops*. You'll be fine."

"Again, where are we going?"

"Again, dinner."

She looked out over the bow at Mockhorn Bay. "I don't know these waters."

"Fortunately, I do, and I won't let you turn *Wave Dancer* into *Sand Dancer*. Ow!" Cam had knuckle punched him in the shoulder.

"In that case, smartass, swap places." She moved over behind the wheel as Rut walked around behind the lean seat and over to the spot she'd vacated.

Rut started flipping switches and adjusting screens on the console, turning on the radar, GPS, and the digital depth finder. He told Cam, "Okay, give her some throttle."

"How much?"

"Thirty-five hundred rpm to start. That'll move us along nicely as you get used to how she handles."

"How fast is she wide open?" Cam asked.

"Should be fifty-eight miles per hour at fifty-five hundred rpm. But we'll take it nice and easy until we get out in the ocean. We'll take Sand Shoal Channel around Mockhorn Island and down to South Bay then over to Red Drum Drain." He showed her the course they'd take on the screen that was linked to the GPS plotter which was logging their trip. "You said you met Daniels, and his place is almost on the way so I'll point it out as we go by. You'll understand a lot more about him when you see it."

"Fine, so long as we don't have to get downwind."

He laughed. "Yeah, his hygiene leaves a bit to be desired."

"I'd rather put up with your paint smell."

"Hey, the deck came out okay, didn't it? It's a small price to pay."

"Right, Michelangelo, I'll try to remember that."

Cammie pushed both throttles forward, and the deep-vee hull rose up out of the water as *Wave Dancer* gained speed. Rut watched Cam carefully, making sure she was comfortable at the helm. He was happy to see her periodically scanning the engine gauges, rather than just relying on the warning horns. She was obviously very experienced with boats. But what made him even happier was seeing the smile on her face. And with the four-stroke engines being so much quieter than their old two-stroke counterparts, at this speed it was easy to hold a conversation without having to yell.

"How's it feel?" he asked her.

"Like you'll have to pry this wheel out of my cold, dead hands. She's a *dream* to run, Rut! Thank you for letting me take the helm on the inaugural trip. Where was it you said we were going?"

"Dinner. But nice try." He laughed.

"Uh, the captain kind of needs a course direction."

"After I show you Daniels's place, we'll go out New Inlet between Daniels's Godwin Island and Wreck Island. Once we get out in the ocean, we'll hang a left. That specific enough for you?"

"No, but at least it's better than what I had to work with before, which was nothing." She feigned a scowl, while still watching out ahead. They followed the channel around Mockhorn down to Red Drum Drain, then turned toward New Inlet.

"Daniels has his own channel that he uses to cut through Mockhorn Island, which takes a mile or two out of the run between his place and my boatyard. But it's very narrow and snakes around through the marsh. If we had tried it, she might've turned into *Marsh Dancer*. It was safer taking this long way around in the deep channels."

Cam nodded, "Deep water is a good thing. *Wave Dancer*, remember?"

"Yeah, I got it." He chuckled, then continued. "Daniels's family has owned Godwin Island for generations. But he's the last of the line. The state wanted to take Godwin to add to the park, and they tried to force Daniels off his land. But he hired a big law firm and fought back."

Cam looked confused, "How could he afford some expensive law firm?"

"Don't let the fact he lives like a hermit throw you; like I said, he's the last of his family's line. He has a pile of money that was left to him, as well as his island. Probably not a Casey-and-Dawn-sized pile, but not an ant hill, either. Anyway, the state all of a sudden realized they had hooked a whale with a hand line, and decided it would be smarter to cut him a sweetheart deal. He got another small pile of dough, as well as the right to live out his days on the island while being left completely alone by the state."

"You admire him, don't you, Rut?"

"How could I not? Fight the state and win, live life the way you want to without being pushed around, seems to me that's pretty similar to what some great folks aspired to back in the 1700s. Unfortunately, somewhere along the way we've lost that aspiration as a people, and now it's more of a rare thing. Which is a damn shame. Speaking of which, there's one more thing I forgot to tell you." Rut explained about the undeclared part of the sales price of his boat sales. "I know the state would call it tax evasion, but they're still getting plenty out of each deal. There's something about it that chaps my butt when they think they have the right to continually tax things that were already bought and paid for. If I can help people lower their rates a bit, I'll do it. Boat owners pay enough taxes as it is. There's the annual boat registration tax, fishing license fee for the state, federal waters fishing license fee, fuel tax, all of it on top of the personal property tax. Buy new outboard engines? That gets reported to the state by the dealer, and you'll get a whopping addition to that personal property tax every year. So while I didn't have a real problem with getting out of the hot marine electronics and fishing gear business, this isn't something I'm going to give up. I figure the little bit that it takes out of the general revenue fund is less than they would've wasted or stolen for themselves anyway. Okay, I'll get off my soapbox now."

Cam looked amused, "Did I say I thought you should? To me, it's one thing when you help a robber steal from honest people, but it's an entirely different thing when it comes to taxation. So many politicians get rich without ever holding a real job at any point in their lives. Insider trading, bribes disguised as book deal advances, huge fees for speeches that say nothing but are designed just to give them cover while they line their pockets with cash. Let them come do my job for a week, and take some of the abuse I do. Or let them suck in paint fumes and get their fingertips worn down by sandpaper, restoring boats like you. What you used to do and what you're doing now are two entirely different things. I've got no problem with this. Especially if it pays for dinner. Where did you say we're eating again?"

Rut nudged her in the ribs as she smiled. Then he pointed over to their right, at an island that was mostly marsh with a few channels, and a comma-shaped strip of beach that bordered New Inlet and the Atlantic Ocean.

"That's Godwin. See that two-story shack out over the water on that little bay? That's Daniels's place."

Even at this distance she could see it was made up of several different types of materials, mostly flotsam and jetsam that he'd found on his beach. The shack looked like it had been continually added onto in phases through the years. The roofs were made of a collection of old corrugated steel sheets, asphalt shingles, and blue tarps. A breakwater wharf made from old railroad ties and rocks extended out from the shack, offering protection for his old *Carolina Skiff* which was moored on the lee side. A hand-painted wooden sign at the end read in huge letters, "Fresh Bait."

Cam said, "I guess if he didn't have any money, we'd call him a crazy hermit. But since he's loaded, this just makes him eccentric."

"That's about the size of it. Probably doesn't need to run the bait business for an income; it's something he just likes doing."

"Don't tell me, let me guess, it's all non-reported cash."

Rut looked thoughtful, "You know, I never asked him. But I'm sure he can't escape the taxes on the income from what he inherited and what the state paid him. There's a paper trail for all that. And his bait business income probably pales in comparison. But he's tight with his money. Know that funny purple-colored bottom paint on his skiff?" When Cam nodded, he said, "That's because I had a couple of half-empty cans of different colors left over from other boats. He wouldn't spring for a new, full gallon of either of them, and talked me down on the price for both. Then had us mix the two together and use it. Said the barnacles might even hate the color more." He laughed.

They went out New Inlet, splitting the distance between the two large and often shifting sandbar beaches on both Godwin and Wreck Islands. Rut saw Cam read the water well, finding the deepest part of the channel. As soon as they hit the ocean, they left the one-foot chop back in the protected inland waters and transitioned into the four-foot ocean swells. Cam headed straight into them for half a mile before turning north and paralleling the narrow strip of beach on the barrier islands.

"I've so missed doing this, Rut. I love running boats, and I love looking at all these miles of deserted beaches. And the way *Dancer* handles these swells is... amazing!"

"Yeah, she's great while she's running. But slow down to trolling speed in this trough and her deep vee will roll you like you're in a barrel. Uses a third more fuel than a flat bottom or a modified vee, but there's nothing more comfortable when you're running. And you've got about twenty miles to run like this. Go ahead and kick her up to forty-five hundred rpm."

"Aha! A clue. That would take us up near Wachapreague." She glanced over at him, grinning as she looked for confirmation.

"Wachapreague Inlet, yes. Wachapreague proper? No. We'll go in the inlet and into Horseshoe Lead, Big Wye Channel, and Blackrock Reach into Burton's Bay."

"Burton's Bay? The *Bluffs*? We're going to the *Bluffs* for dinner! You know, I've never been there before."

"Casey and Dawn bought that property right after *Bayside*. Same food as at *Bayside*, but in a much more casual atmosphere, and much lower prices. Last night Casey told me they wanted to create a place where people who worked around the water could afford to eat there, but that had the same quality as *Bayside*, and that's why they built it."

"Nice! You know, you're really spoiling me, taking me to dinner all the time," she said.

"That's my plan. See, if I cooked anything other than on my grill, you'd run off into the night in terror. Except breakfast. I make great cereal."

Cam rolled her eyes. "Is this your way of asking if I'd cook you a meal?"

"No, just my own version of a verbal consumer warning label."

"I'll cook you a meal."

"That would be spoiling *me*. Then I might want you to stick around."

"That's *my* plan. Though I wasn't really planning on going anywhere, kinda hoping you'd like me to stick around. You said I was still a work in progress, remember? I figure I need to be close by for that."

"I did, didn't I? And yes, you do."

⁓

As Rut and Cammie were sitting down at the *Bluffs*, Dawn was sitting across from Casey in the salon of *Lady Dawn*, rereading the *Handbook for Federal Grand Jurors*. "As much as this is going to be an ongoing pain in the butt, it might be interesting as well. But I wish it was a single three-day stint instead of twelve of them."

Casey looked up from a report he was reading. "It does seem like a lot of time taken out of the daily lives of each juror."

"A tenth of a year! And only because we live in the Eastern District. If we lived in the Western District over by Charlottesville, they only do two days a month for six months. A much better deal."

"Sounds like it."

Dawn said, "And secrecy is a big part of this. By oath, we're not allowed to ever discuss anything that happened in the grand jury, even afterward. Not to anyone, even spouses."

"That's harsh. We've never had secrets from each other before."

"I don't have any choice. But I do get immunity for anything I do within the scope of the grand jury duty."

"That's... different. What could you possibly need to do within that scope which might require immunity?"

"I have no clue. But apparently it's been part of it since the very beginning, like the secrecy part. And they suggest we not say anything to anyone about being on the grand jury so no 'target' could find out and get to any of us to sway votes. There are supposed to be twenty-three jurors, with sixteen needed for a quorum, and twelve votes are necessary for a 'true bill' to issue an indictment. So, if only sixteen show up, and five of them won't vote to indict somebody, it's like the other eleven don't count and those no-shows are voting no. But this is just about sending a case to trial, or giving the investigators more power to investigate people. You'd think it would be a simple majority of whoever shows up."

"About that secrecy thing, you haven't told anyone about being summoned, right?"

"Just Lindsay. I opened the envelope when I was at lunch with her, but she won't say anything. So, there's nothing to worry about. Oh, and Cammie. But I'm sure I can trust her, too. Especially after what she shared with me. She said Rut and I, and now you, are the only ones who know she killed her rapist, a man who was undoubtedly going to kill her. Put me on *that* jury, and I'll make sure she's acquitted."

Casey said, "Sounds like she already put you on it. You like her, don't you." It wasn't a question.

"Don't you? I mean, how could you not. And Rut seems to make a habit of helping people. She's lucky to have found him, he's obviously good for her. Seeing those two together, you'd think they've been dating for years. Heck, *I* feel like I've known them for years."

"Oh, I think they'll be around from now on. At least I hope they will. And now we need to talk about making sure they are..."

## 11

# THE OFFER

The next day, Frankie Hicks slid into the usual booth across from Mango. "The chick's name is Dawn Shaw. She and Casey, her old man, are loaded. There ain't gonna be no way ta bribe her. You'll have ta take another route with this one or find somebody else ta flip that jury. I tried ta follow her home, but they got some kinda private compound over next ta *Mallard Cove*. Fence, woods blockin' the view, the works. Maybe cameras, I don't know. I'm thinkin' maybe we can see somethin' from the water on your boat."

"I don't know who else is gonna be on that jury, so forget about somebody else. By the time we find out, I'll be indicted. And you mean you wanna use the boat that's got my name plastered all across the ass end? What part ah 'I don't want nothin' connectin' me to this' didn't you get?"

"Sorry, Mango."

"Well, make sure ya don't forget again. I got an idea. You said they got woods, right? Well, I got that little drone I mess around with. Great camera on it, and it's real quiet. You can fly it over there and see where she goes, and what time her old man leaves. I'm startin' ta get an idea. And I want ya ta keep tabs on Rut, too. I don't know if this grand jury thing has anything ta do with him. I don't think it does, 'cause he'd go down with me if he rats me out, unless he got himself immunity, the prick. Says he's got some kinda insurance policy on our marine gear business, and I want ta get it away from him. Maybe there'd be somethin' he'd be willin' ta trade for it. We need ta figure that one out. Get Joey ta look around his place when Rut's at work. If we can grab it, I don't need ta trade for it. But tell that numbskull ta make sure he don't get caught. I don't wanna tip Rut off."

"I'll take care of it, Mango."

∼

CAMMIE AND ANGEL were working the brunch/lunch shift together since it was Sunday. The place was packed from the moment they opened, as the *Beach Bar's* Sunday Seafood Brunch was famous around ESVA. It meant great tips, and that there was no time for Angel to bug Cam for news on the Rut front. She did pause for a moment mid-afternoon when Dawn stopped by and waved her over, inviting her to drop by *C2* after work to have a drink and kick back a bit before she headed home.

"First you land Rut, and are keeping all closed-lipped about it. Now you're getting tight with the boss too? I suppose you won't tell me what that's about, either."

"Technically, she's not our boss, Angel. She's one of a group of investors. Murph and Lindsay are the real 'bosses,' since they own the majority of the place."

"Oh, and I suppose you and Rut are hanging with all of them now."

"I'm not even planning to see Rut today."

"Trouble in paradise already?" She almost sneered at Cam.

"No, but what is your problem?"

"I don't have one, but you do. You've changed ever since you started doing the 'horizontal mambo' with Rut. I don't know what's happening with you, and I feel left out."

"I'm just busy, that's all. But I do like keeping the details of my private life, well, private."

"This is *me*, Cammie! I tell you everything about my life!"

"Yeah, and there's a lot of it that I've asked you not to."

"Fine! I'll find somebody else who'll listen and appreciate what I tell 'em." She turned on a heel and stormed off, ignoring Cammie for the rest of their shift.

RATHER THAN LEAVE her car in the parking lot and get interrogated tomorrow about where she went and who was she with, Cammie drove over to C2, parking behind the boathouse next to a sporty little European convertible. Up at the pool, Dawn was sitting with two beautiful women who looked to be between Dawn and Cammie's ages. One was tall, very toned, with short-cropped, naturally platinum blond hair and stunning ice-blue eyes. She introduced herself as Rikki Jenkins and introduced the other woman as her partner, Cindy Crenshaw. She was an inch or two shorter, very shapely with below-the-shoulder curly blond hair and bluish-gray eyes. Cam had heard of Cindy, who was the head of the Shaws' hospitality group.

Dawn poured Cam a white wine, which the three of them were already drinking, and motioned for her to take a seat. "I wanted you all to get a chance to meet. Cam, Rikki and Cindy are good friends of Casey's and mine, as well as members of our 'no tan lines' bunch. You'll be seeing them around C2 quite a bit. Rik is Casey's favorite fishing partner."

Rikki said, "I wouldn't say favorite, but we wet a hook or two together quite a bit."

Dawn said, "She and Sandy are teaching Missy, Eric's daughter, some of the finer points of angling."

Cindy asked, "Do you fish, Cammie?"

"Please call me Cam. I used to, but I haven't in years. In fact, I ran an outboard last night for the first time in a decade. I'd forgotten how much fun it was."

"Well, you're in the right place now, we've got a bunch of them around here you can run. We'll put together a girl's fishing trip soon," Dawn said. "And just wait until *Sharke* gets here next month. Casey and Eric are down in North Carolina checking on her progress right now. They should be back in a half-hour or so."

"Fishing with you guys would be a ball. I'm hoping that Rut asks me to fish with him some, too."

"If he doesn't, you can count on us. But I'm willing to bet he will," Dawn said.

Rik and Cindy stayed another twenty minutes, then headed home to their boat, which they live on at *Bayside*. They'd stopped by on their way back from spending the day in Virginia Beach after Dawn said she wanted them to meet Cam.

"Rikki didn't tell you about her work. She's the majority partner in a security firm that handles, among other things, government security problems. She's one of the other women besides you that I call a badass. If she likes you, she'll have your back from now on, and trust me, she liked you."

"She seemed pretty... uh... quiet and tough? I thought I hadn't made all that great an impression."

"Yeah, that's her way, and yes, you did. Like I said, trust me."

They heard the sound of a helicopter approaching. Dawn looked off in the distance and said, "Ah, Casey's home."

Eric's Sikorsky S-76 was approaching from the south. When Casey told Rut about it, he hadn't mentioned it was a huge, sleek, nine-passenger flying office and living room. They both watched as the pilot settled it gently onto the pad. Eric, Casey, and a young teenaged girl emerged from the passenger cabin and hurried over to them as they stood up.

"Aunt Dawn, you should see *Sharke* now! She's coming along so well, and I can't wait until she's in the water in a few weeks. Oh, hi, you must be Miss Pinder." She held out her hand to shake Cammie's. "I'm Elaina Clarke, but my friends and family call me Missy, so please do."

Cam was impressed. "Well Missy, my name is Cammie, but my friends call me Cam, so I hope you will too."

Missy beamed, "Cam it is! We were just down in Beaufort,

checking on a boat my dad and Uncle Casey are building. Do you fish?"

"I was just telling Dawn that I used to."

"*Sharke* is going to be the best sportfisherman ever! Here are some pictures." She pulled up the pictures on a tablet she was carrying. The boat looked huge.

"How big is she?" Cam asked.

"Seventy-five feet! She's going to be so stable."

"Pretty flat aft, so she should be."

"SeaKeeper gyro, too! It'll be like fishing from the dock on even the roughest days. You'll have to come out with us."

Cam wasn't sure what a SeaKeeper was, but not really wanting to admit it, she said, "Nice!"

Eric and Casey walked up and said hello. Eric said, "I see you were cornered and got the full rundown on *Sharke*." Cam could hear in his voice the pride he had in his daughter.

"Not cornered; interested. Beautiful boat, and a very bright young lady."

Missy beamed at the compliment. "I was telling Cam that she has to fish with us."

Eric nodded. "I agree." He and Missy hung out a few more minutes before leaving to meet Candi at *Bayside*.

After the pair left, Casey poured himself a glass of wine and sat with the women. "So where's Rut? I thought you two were joined at the hip."

Cam blushed slightly, "Not really. I worked today, and he went over to Virginia Beach to pick up a few things and grab dinner. I have the evening shift tomorrow, so I probably won't see him for a few days."

Dawn said, "Good, then you are free to have dinner with us tonight on the boat." When Cam looked hesitant, she said, "We're not taking no for an answer. There's someone else we want you to meet over dinner."

"You've been the topic of conversation around here these past few days," Casey said. "In fact, you were on the flight back as well."

"Which explains how Missy knew my last name."

Casey nodded. "We want to do something for you for helping save Dawn."

"I didn't save her, Rut did."

"Felt to me like a team effort," Dawn argued. "Here's the thing, Rut has his own business, so there's not much we can do for him that he isn't already doing himself. But we were wondering if you'd like to work in our company. You're bright, stable, and have a great way with people. I think you would be a great fit on our team, and there's a lot of future opportunities within our business as well. But that all depends on if you're willing to leave the *Cove Beach Bar*."

"So, it's another server position in one of your other restaurants?"

Dawn said, "No. Let me explain what we have in mind..."

RUT TURNED on the porch light and whipped open his front door, irritated yet anxious to see who was pounding on it after eleven o'clock at night. This was the first time since he and Cammie had started seeing each other that he had gotten to sleep at a decent hour, and now that was blown to hell. He was surprised to see a flushed-looking Cammie standing in the doorway. "Can I come in?"

"Uh, sure. Is everything okay?" He backed up, leaving her room to pass. But instead of brushing by, she wrapped her arms around him and kissed him passionately. He smelled wine on her breath as she said, "Show me those tan sheets you were talking about."

A while later, as they lay there in the dark, completely spent, he asked, "At the risk of wrecking the mood, do you mind if I ask what brought this on? I may want to remember it at some point down the road when I might need it."

"For somebody else, or for me?" She was only half-joking. She had come there to find answers for herself.

"Whoa! That sure came out of left field."

She propped herself up on an elbow. "And you didn't answer my question."

Even in the dim moonlight coming through the bedroom window

he could see the concern on her face. "There isn't anyone else, you know that."

"Is there likely to be?"

"Where are you going with this, Cam?"

She sighed. "I need to make a decision about something, and I like getting all the input I can before I do. I know we just started going out, but is this only fun and games, or what?"

"Yeah, we did just start going out, and I don't have a crystal ball. I can tell you that I'm not interested in getting married again, if that's what you're asking. But fun and games? Is that what it feels like to you?"

"I'm asking you, remember?"

"Then no, it doesn't. It isn't 'hit and run,' or 'sport sex," at least not to me. This isn't all about sex; I care about you. I think about you during the day, and I enjoy spending time with you and not just when we're sweating up my sheets. You know that you've had more helm time on my new-to-me boat than I have. I'd say that's a pretty good start to a relationship. But that's only my opinion, and it takes more than just mine to go there."

"So, you want a relationship."

"I thought we already have one, so yeah, I guess I do. But if I'm wrong, or way off base, tell me now before this goes any farther."

"Right now, my job schedule kind of screws things up, since sometimes I have to work on the weekends and nights when you're off. It could make going any further kind of tough."

"I'm willing to try working around it. But it's starting to sound like you aren't, and more like you came over here to say goodbye. I hope I'm wrong."

"No, I just wanted your take on things. The Shaws offered me a job with their real estate management and acquisition company tonight. I'd be working from their office building at *Mallard Cove*. Mostly Monday through Friday, but sometimes there'll be a Saturday or some longer days when there's a push on, but then some Fridays off to make up for the extra hours. They say they work hard, and play just as hard. The starting pay is about two and a half times what I'm making at the restaurant."

"That sounds great, but what do you know about real estate?"

"About as much as the woman who would be my boss, Kari Denton, did when she joined the company, and now she runs that division. The Shaws trained her, and they've offered to train me, too. I'd be her field assistant. I met her on their boat tonight."

"What did you tell them?"

"I said I needed the night to think about it."

"You have an interesting way of thinking."

She poked him in the ribs. "Very funny. I'm serious. I want to get your take on it."

He pulled her over closer to him. "I think you should do whatever makes you happy. Making more money is great, but not if you're bored or miserable."

"I'm starting to be bored and miserable at the *Beach Bar*. But I need to know if you'll want to spend more time together if our schedules are more alike."

"Duh! Yes. We just got a new boat that needs running, there are fish that need catching, and barrier islands that need exploring."

"I like the sound of all that."

"Sleep on it tonight."

"Let's sleep later."

## 12

# A VISITOR

Thanks to the earlier start to getting some sleep, at least before it was interrupted, Rut managed to get fully rested before getting up and going to work. Almost. Kissing Cam goodbye as she lay in bed, he asked her to call him later and let him know how things went with the Shaws. Then she settled back in for another hour or so of sleep. After she got up, once again she helped herself to one of his longer tee shirts, then went into the kitchen to make her breakfast and turn on the stereo.

IT WAS an hour past the opening of Rut's boatyard. Joey crept through the brush next to the overgrown gravel road where he'd stashed his pickup. He could see the roof of Rut's house ahead, just above the bushes. Cautiously and quietly, he made his way up to the side of the house. Peering in the edge of a window, he discovered it was in a side wall of Rut's bedroom. Suddenly there was movement inside, and he ducked down to the corner of the window as a nice-looking brunette danced into the room, her body swaying to the beat of a song coming from somewhere deeper in the house. She went through a door that looked like it led into a bathroom. She came back out a minute later with a handful of clothes that she set on the bed. Turning away from the window, she pulled the tee shirt off over her head, leaving her bare backside in full view while still moving to the music.

"Damn," Joey thought to himself, "*That bitch is older but way better lookin' than any of them skanks at the strip club. What a great butt! C'mon baby, turn around an' quit teasin' me. Show me whatcha got...*" Cam bent over to step into her panties. Joey felt his face go flush as he thought, "*C'mon, bend over a little farther, you teasin' bitch!*" Much to his frustration, Cam sat down on the edge of the bed still facing away from him as she pulled up her shorts.

Joey knew that Mango said to make sure he wasn't seen, but if he was here right now, he'd understand why he just couldn't do that. No way he could resist this bitch. Joey tried the window and found that it raised a little bit when he tried it. He knew the music would cover the noise of him climbing through. Joey was sure she wouldn't know he was there until he climbed up across the bed and pulled her down from behind, covering her mouth so she couldn't scream. He hoped she was a fighter, he really loved it when they fought back...

"Hey! Get away from there you sumbitch!" Joey turned and looked out over the water where some old man in a scow was pulling up to the seawall to dock. He turned and shouted toward the haul out slip, "Hey, Big Jim! Some asshole is breakin' into Rut's house!"

Joey turned and fled into the scrub, hoping to get away before Rut might have a chance to see and recognize him. The old man had gotten a good look at him though, there was no getting around that.

Big Jim came running across the yard, with Rut right on his heels. Daniels yelled from his boat, "The sumbitch was openin' the side window! Took off that way through the scrub!" He pointed at the overgrown property next door to Rut's house. They ran over to the property line but heard the sound of a motor starting and a vehicle peeling out on gravel. The guy had gotten away. Rut rushed back over to his front door, bursting through it. Cammie was just pulling her own shirt on. She looked at him, startled.

"Did you get a look at him?" Rut asked, breathlessly.

"Him who? What are you talking about?"

"The guy who was breaking in! Damn it, hold on." He went over to the living room and turned the stereo off, then he went back toward the bedroom where Cam was coming through the door with a concerned look on her face. He went past her into the bedroom and over to the window. She followed him.

"What guy who was breaking in?"

"Did you open this window?"

"What? No! What are you saying?"

"This window always stays closed, but I must not have locked it. Somebody was opening it, and Daniels spotted him from his boat and frightened him off."

The color rose in her face as she realized he had been right behind her, watching as she was getting dressed. "I never even heard him over the music." She started shaking as the old memory came back to haunt her. But it wasn't fear, it was rage over the violation of this home where she'd shared so much of both her past and herself with Rut. Up until now it had been a place where she'd felt both comfortable and safe.

Rut walked over to the bedside table and reached behind it, pulling out a Glock 19 pistol from a hidden holster. He handed it to her, "Fifteen shots in the magazine, and one in the breech. No safety. Pull the trigger; it's ready to go bang. Draw up and fire from their knees to their head, and don't stop shooting until they stop moving. Get familiar with where it stays."

Her rage was still boiling up to the surface. "*Here.* Some son of a bitch was breaking in *here.*"

"Could've been that kid, coming back for revenge, who knows. I'm going to go ask Daniels what he saw."

Cam paused a minute as it sank in that it was Daniels who had spotted the guy. She said, "Yeah quick, before he comes in here and his scent follows him." She smirked, thinking about how it would've been great to catch the bastard and lock him up in a small room with Daniels. Rut looked curious at the way she was now smiling, wondering what could've prompted it. But he was glad to see her calm down a bit at this point, as her rage began fading.

Outside, he spotted Daniels talking to Big Jim over by the seawall. "Did you get a good look at him, Daniels?"

"Damn right I did. I'd know that sumbitch if I ever saw him again." He looked past Rut as Cam came through the door. "Oh god, don't tell me she was in there by herself."

"Yeah. Was this guy a kid? Maybe late teens?"

"Naw, more like early to mid-thirties, black hair, short li'l sumbitch, but built like a tank. Never seen him before. But I'm gonna whip his ass, I see him again."

"No, I want you to promise to call me if you see him. I've got a few questions to ask him." His eyes narrowed and his lips tightened.

"Best way ta get answers, Rut, is ta take that sumbitch for a boat ride with plenty ah anchor chain wrapped around his legs. Scare the piss out'n him. Oh, sorry, ma'am." He realized Cam was now also within hearing range.

She waved her hand, dismissing the language. "No problem, it's that kind of morning."

He nodded, "Yeah, I guess that'd be so."

Big Jim asked, "Daniels, did you just take a bath?"

The elder man looked sheepish. "Fell in yesterday. Probably take another week or so ta build back some a my mosquito immunity. Bastards'll eat me alive outside 'til then. Oops, sorry again, ma'am."

Cam hid a smile as Big Jim chuckled. "Lotsa garlic. It'll do da same thin'."

"Really? That'll work? Rub it on?" Daniels looked skeptical.

"Roast it, an eat um whole after they get kinda soft 'n' squishy. Gotta eat enough so's it comes out thru da skin tho'. Least a couple a heads. You'll see."

"Well, I was goin' ta th' grocery, so I'll take ya up on your suggestion, Jim. Save my skin twix now an' a few weeks, at least 'til I get my full immunity back."

Jim nodded, "It'll be workin' by late tonight."

DANIELS DROVE off and Jim went back to the boatyard as Rut walked Cam back to the house to get her car keys. She glanced sideways at him, "You don't have to guard me you know. I can handle myself."

"Believe me, I know that."

"When Daniels described him, you looked like you might've known who he was."

"Not for certain, but he *might* be one of Mango's goons. I don't want to scare you, but just be aware of your surroundings. And if you spot somebody following you in your car or when you're out walking around, call me. It might be a good idea for you to move over here with me for a while, too."

"Isn't it a little early in this new relationship of ours for me to be moving in?" She smirked at him.

"I'm serious. I don't want something to happen to you because of me. I'd never forgive myself for it. There's safety in numbers."

"Rut, that's apparently what this was. I'm not the one who recognized his description, so I doubt he came here looking for me. You're the one who needs to watch his back."

"Please, Cam, humor me."

She sighed, "All right, I will. Might be a nice test run; I can see how you'll react when you see all my stuff that lives on the bathroom counter." She grinned slyly.

Rut's eyes glazed over for a second as that thought sunk in, but he quickly shook it off. "Good. Thank you, I'll feel better knowing you're here."

"Well, we're about to see if that's true. Big difference between staying overnight every now and then and moving in, even just for a little while."

CAM PARKED in the marina lot, then walked through the gate and over to *Lady Dawn*. Casey and Dawn were aboard, working from home. Casey had built his real estate business down in Florida while living and working aboard his earlier boats. Now he and Dawn kept the same habit here in Virginia, though they also worked sometimes from *C2*. They each had offices at *Bayside* and *Mallard Cove*, but they saved those for meetings with their teams. Dawn let Cam into the salon after she knocked, and got her a cup of coffee before they settled onto a couch together. Casey sat across from them. He said, "I liked that you didn't jump at our offer, and wanted some time to think it over. Now I'm hoping I'll like the answer just as much."

Cam said, "I hope you do, too, since I'd like to accept it if it's still open."

"That's great, Cam! I think we'll all enjoy working with each other," Dawn replied.

"I just need to give my two weeks' notice today."

"Um, about that, in the hopes that you'd say 'yes,' I already talked to your manager, just in case. Since you're going to a related company, five days is all she needs to find a replacement, and I'll take care of notifying her for you. You can start with us on Monday. Do you have any 'business casual' clothes?"

Cam hadn't thought about that, and shook her head, "No, but I'll get some."

Casey handed her a check. "Here's a signing bonus which should cover that."

She was surprised, especially at the amount. "Do you give everyone such a hefty signing bonus?"

Dawn replied, "A few. The ones with the most promise. We've been right every time so far; they're all still with us."

WHEN CAM WALKED into the *Beach Bar*, she discovered that news traveled faster than she walked. She was met with a frosty stare from Angel. "You know, I never thought of you before as a brown-nosing suck-up."

Cam's eyes narrowed. "Then why would you start now?"

"Because you've earned it. Leaving here to go to a corporate job with the Shaws? You're trading your freedom so you can become a stiff. If I'd have known this is what Rut would turn you into, I'd have never sicced him on ya."

Cam sputtered as her anger rose, "Rut... turned me into... sicced him on *me*? First off, nobody turns me into anything. I make my own way, deciding things for myself. And if you'll recall, *I* asked *him* out, so just who was sicced on whom? Secondly, I was offered that job by the Shaws, I didn't ask for it, but I damn sure wasn't about to turn it down. You're five years older than me. Ever notice how you have to hustle so much harder now to make the same tips you used to back when you were in your twenties, when your boobs were perkier and your butt was firmer? Have your feet started aching by the end of your shifts? What do you think it'll be like for you ten years from now? If you had been given this opportunity, you should've jumped on it like I did. And if you were really my friend, you'd be happy for me instead of jealous."

"Jealous? Of getting a job as a stiff? Give me a break. Maybe you are going to be getting off your feet, but then again, maybe getting on your back was part of the deal."

Cam wasn't going to get lured farther into a public fight with Angel, so she turned and walked off. But Frankie Hicks had seen and heard the whole row from his table and knew an opportunity when he saw one. So, that brunette is getting with Rut these days, that was one very valuable piece of information. So was the fact that she would now be working for the Shaws.

Hicks then chatted up Angel every time she came over to check on him. He put a fifty on the table, to eventually cover a check that would be way less than half of that. A fact that wasn't lost on Angel, who became friendlier and started leaning over farther and exposing more cleavage when bringing his refills and clearing his dishes. Hicks left her all the change from that fifty, just as the real lunch rush began. He headed over to fly the drone from the woods in the state park beyond *C2*, mapping out what lay beyond the fence. Then he'd come back during the mid-afternoon lull, ordering an expensive drink and putting an even larger bill on the table. Money talks, and it also makes people talk. He was counting on a nice conversation and a lot of information coming out of Angel.

## 13

# REDECORATING

The next day, Frankie Hicks met Mango early at the deli to give him a report. He started with what he'd overheard in the *Cove Beach Bar*.

"You're sure that waitress is Rut's girlfriend?" Mango asked.

"Yeah, Cammie somethin', and now she's a pal of the Shaws', too. Been hangin' around with 'em, and about to go work for 'em," Frankie replied.

"Good ta know. So, what did you get from the drone?"

Hicks said, "Nice layout. The Shaws live on a big yacht, but he spent a lot of time over by the pool today." He handed Mango a tablet with some stored drone footage.

"Nice ta be him, huh? Wow, that redhead's his wife?" Some of the footage showed Dawn at the pool with Casey.

"Uh-huh."

"Yowsa. That is one well-built babe. Like I said, it's good ta be Shaw... or, it was." He grinned at Hicks. "That pool area is nice and close ta the boat channel. What's all that concrete between it and the pool?"

"Seaplane ramp and a helipad."

"Huh. If we could grab him at the pool, we could take him out by boat. We just need ta know if he keeps a schedule, and what it is. Keep watchin' him. Make sure he don't spot the drone." Mango instructed.

"I been flying it extra high. But there's a tiki tower kinda thing I can sneak up in and watch from, so I won't need it much."

"Good. Get back on it. And whatta ya hear from Joey?"

Hicks looked uncomfortable. "He ran into a little problem up there. Rut's girlfriend was home, and some guy in a boat saw him tryin' ta get inta the place."

Mango exploded, "Damn it! I shoulda known better than to let you send that idiot. So now Rut'll have put two and two together and be watching out around his place. Knowin' him, he'll make sure his insurance policy ain't there anymore, if it was ever there in the first place. But the girlfriend, she could be the leverage we need, just like Shaw. Okay, keep watchin' Shaw's place. The more we know, the better plan we can come up with. My 'thing' happens a week from tomorrow, which means we gotta have him a week from today. This is gonna be tight."

"Yeah."

~

CAM PULLED up next to Rut's house and saw him sitting out on the porch next to a cooler. As she walked up the steps, he reached into the cooler and pulled out a bottle of *Starr Hill's Ramble On*, handing it to her and getting a kiss in return. As she sat down she said, "A girl could get used to this you know."

"The beer, or sitting on the porch after work?"

"The whole shebang."

"Well, from your text, it sounded like it was a rough day. I knew that woman could have a mean streak when she wanted to. It might've been part of why we didn't last."

"Yeah." Cam wasn't pleased to be reminded about his past with Angel. "But she'd never turned it on me before. Now I can't wait to be out of there. They already hired my replacement. I'm training her the rest of the week, then I'm done."

"I thought you needed to give them two weeks?" He was surprised.

"Dawn arranged it. I guess they wanted me in their office sooner. Speaking of which, I need to go clothes shopping over in Norfolk to get some new work duds."

"Have fun with that."

"I figured I'd buy you dinner at *Frederick's Steak House* if you come with me."

Rut was surprised; *Frederick's* was as expensive as *Rooftops*. "What? Did you rob the till on the way out of the bar tonight?"

"Signing bonus." She beamed.

"I didn't know you played pro ball."

"You'd think so from the check size. C'mon, let's get a shower then we'll go."

"I've already had mine."

She shot him a look that made him rethink what he'd just said. "Did you miss the part about 'let's'? As in, let us *both* grab a shower? Plural? You were right, it was a crappy day and I want to turn it around starting right now."

He took another sip of his beer and set it down. "I guess a man can never be too clean. I'd hate to start smelling like Daniels."

∼

"That was one great meal. It was even worth coming along while you shopped for clothes."

"Well, you didn't look too bored when I was trying on bikinis," Cam said, with a seductive smile.

"Yeah, about that, I didn't know that swimwear qualified as 'work duds.'"

"Dawn suggested I leave one at *C2*, in case I want to take a dip sometimes after work. Another perk of working for them."

Rut replied, "Yeah, well, I have pool privileges too, and I'm not even on salary."

"Speaking of which, now that I'm hiding out at your place, I guess we'll be doing even more things together, right?"

"Cam, I have to start getting more sleep..."

"Funny guy. No, I mean now that we both have most weekends off together, do you want to make plans for this weekend?"

"Sure. Do you mind if they include using the boat?" Rut asked.

"That's up to you, it's your boat."

"Yeah, but it's *our* weekend. If you want us to do something in the boat, all you have to do is say so."

"Hey, twist my arm! I'm always up for a boat ride." She started looking pensive, "I've been thinking..."

He interrupted her, "Nothing good could come from that." Cam swatted his arm. "Hey! I'm driving!"

"If you don't want to be wrecking instead of driving, don't pick on me."

"Okay, okay! You said you were thinking..."

"Yeah. What do you think about going fishing on Saturday? I heard some guys in the bar talking today, they got into the mahi in a big way, and not that far offshore. They found 'em under a log and a pallet that were on the edge of some seaweed. Couple of big bulls, and some schoolies."

Rut nodded. "Let's check the weather on Friday, but heck yes. Fresh mahi is one of my favorite foods."

"Sautéed, or fried?"

"Have you forgotten the part about the only thing that I don't cook on the grill is cereal?"

"This works out. You do the outside cooking, and I'll cook inside. I make a mean Mahi à la Française."

"I don't even know what that means, but I'm liking the sound of it already."

"Trust me, you'll love it."

They pulled up to Rut's house when he suddenly said, "Stop! Don't get out of the truck. I locked that door when we left, and now it's ajar. Stay here, I'll be right back. If you see anybody, lay on the horn and don't let up."

"Where are you going?"

"To get a friend."

"What?!?" But he was already out and running toward his office. She hit the lock button. In a minute and a half that seemed like an hour he was back, the .44 magnum pistol from his office in his hand. He motioned for her to stay in the truck, and he went through the front door. There was a bright flash, but she didn't hear the gunshot. Cam bolted out of the truck and through the front door, afraid that someone with a silenced pistol had shot him.

She cried out, "Rut!"

The lights in the kitchen came on, and Rut was standing there, unhurt, but with a finger across his lips warning her to be quiet, and again motioning her to stay put. He advanced across the living room, reached in and turned on the bedroom ceiling light. Sweeping the pistol around the room, then clearing the bathroom, he told her, "Nobody's here." That's when she realized the place had been trashed.

"I thought someone was shooting at you!"

"Nah, the bulb blew on a lamp that was knocked over when I turned on the light switch. Made a bright flash when it let loose." He surveyed the damage. "Somebody was looking for something, but they didn't find it because it wasn't here. Probably your friend from this morning."

"Not *my* friend."

"Okay, your personal peeping Tom. One with a big foot." He motioned to the front door and the splintered doorframe where it had been kicked in.

Cam exclaimed, "I'm glad we weren't here!"

"He knew we weren't. Look how he tried getting in this morning, all quiet and stealthy, knowing you were the only one home. He just didn't know that he'd have been biting off a lot more than he could chew with you. But this," he motioned to the door again, "meant he knew nobody was around to hear it."

"So, he cased the place, or has been watching us."

"I would've, and I'd have been really careful about it, especially after getting run off this morning. Seeing the two of us leaving at that time of day, it's likely he thought we went out to a bar or a restaurant. That's why the mess, and why he kicked in the door, he probably figured we could be back in an hour, not four. If he'd known he had that much time, he probably wouldn't have trashed the place, tipping us off that he had been here. Which reminds me..."

Rut went into the bedroom, reaching behind the bedside table. The drawer had been pulled out and the contents dumped on the bed, but he found the Glock was still in its holster on the back. He held it up for Cam to see. "Yeah, not exactly what you might call a thorough search." After he replaced it, he went over to a picture on the wall that was mounted on a hinge. Behind it was his wall safe, and after opening it he saw that everything was as he'd left it, including the stacks of cash.

"I didn't even know that safe was there," Cam said.

"Luckily he didn't either, or he might've figured what he wanted was in there and stuck around to try forcing me to open it. He'd have been wrong, it's all on a thumb drive that isn't anywhere near here. But I'm surprised he didn't break into my office after that, it would've been the first place I'd have looked. I don't think this guy is all that swift. Probably isn't even sure of what he's looking for."

"I'm just glad he's gone. That, and the fact that we'll have two pistols in here with us tonight."

Rut replied, "Yeah, I think I'll carry my forty-four with me for a while, at least until things settle down."

"Good idea, this guy is a bad combination of two things: bold and stupid."

"I have a great combination answer to that: Smith & Wesson."

## 14

## COMPLICATIONS

The rest of the week passed without any further incident involving either Joey or Angel. Cam arrived at Rut's after her last midday shift on Friday to find him installing a large, oval tank on the deck behind the lean seat in *Wave Dancer*. She hopped down onto the boat as he tightened the last hose clamp on a fitting.

"I like the new portable hot tub," she grinned.

"We'll see how you like it in March when the water's forty degrees," he retorted.

"This thing is huge. What's the plan?"

"You'll see in a few minutes," Rut said as he flipped a switch activating the pump that filled it. "Nothing drives Mahi crazier than live or fresh menhaden, and I heard the bait schools are running along the beach right now. So, we'll go load up on some to use as bait tomorrow, and if we get enough, we can chum with them as well. You go fill up a cooler with a few beers and some water, and I'll grab some rods and my cast net."

"Rods? Are we going fishing now?" Cam asked.

"Anytime I have bait in the boat, I carry at least one rod along, too. I can't think of anything more frustrating than seeing fish, having bait, and nothing to hook either up with."

"Good point. I'll go set up the cooler."

On the way out a few minutes later Cam told him, "By the way, we're invited to a seafood cookout at *C2* tomorrow night if you want to go."

"Sounds like fun. Think they'd mind if we came by boat, and got cleaned up there after fishing?" Rut asked.

"I'm sure they wouldn't, since that's what the place is for, so that's a great plan."

She looked at the wheel then back at Rut as he laughed. "Gee, Cam, would you like to run the boat?"

"I thought you'd never ask!" As she took the wheel, a huge grin now spread across her face. Rut still watched her closely, but saw that she was relying less on the plotter as she learned the channel. When they entered New Inlet, she glanced over at Daniels's place where a small sportfisherman was pulling up to his breakwater. Cam said, "It looks like he's got some business."

Rut glanced over, and she saw his jaw clench. Even though he could barely read the name on the stern at this distance, he definitely recognized the symbol painted next to it, the namesake fruit of *Mangoritaville*. "Yeah, that's Mango. I wish I'd never told him about Daniels. He must be getting ready to go fishing offshore this weekend. Daniels has his 'Fresh Bait' sign out again."

∽

DANIELS DIDN'T HAVE a good feeling about seeing Mango and his crew of goons pulling up, but he didn't have a strong enough bad feeling to refuse to sell them bait, at least not yet. Still, he wasn't overjoyed to see the Ocean Yacht pull up to the breakwater. As he went out to meet them, he saw Mango had a new crew-member with him this time. This was someone he had seen before, but not with Mango.

"You sumbitch! You tried breakin' into my friend's place while his woman was home alone! I'm gonna kick your ass, you little bastard..." Despite Rut's request that he call him instead of confronting the goon, the spry septuagenarian leapt into the cockpit. He landed on the deck with a sickening crunch as a hidden support gave way, and that section of aging fiberglass deck suddenly delaminated. He kept his balance though, and launched himself at the short hoodlum.

Joey recognized Daniels up on the breakwater, and he was ready for him as he hit the deck and charged forward. He pulled a switchblade from his back pocket, releasing the blade as he thrust the handle forward. Daniels saw the knife coming at the last second and tried to evade it, but Joey's reactions were too quick for him. He drove the blade deep into Daniels's stomach, then pulled it back out and drove it in again, this time high in his chest. This second thrust glanced off a rib and sliced through Daniels's aorta. He went down gasping, blood spurting from his chest. The last thing he saw was Mango coming down the flybridge ladder, screaming at the short guy, as his world went dark.

"What the hell did you do that for?!? Have you lost your mind?" Mango screamed at Joey.

"He was the old guy who saw me over at Rut's place. He could identify me. You always said get rid of any loose ends, Mango!"

"Don't you turn this on me, damn it! Too many people know I been buying bait from this ol' man, an' can connect me wit' this place." He held up his hand while he thought, and looked out at the end of the breakwater. "Okay, Mikey, go out there and flip his sign around to the 'Sold Out' side. And you, dumbass," he pointed at Joey, "you dump him overboard and scrub down my deck. Then you go over to dat floating pen an' net up every last tinker mackerel he's got and put 'em in my baitwell. Check the tanks on his boat and the rest of the pens and dump everything else. If anybody comes ta check on him, it's gotta look like the sign was right, an' he just took off with somebody on a fishing trip after he sold outta bait."

"Jeeze, Mango, this guy reeks!" Joey complained. "Can you give me a hand dumpin' him overboard?"

"No! You created the problem and now you're gonna fix it by yourself. Do it!" He watched his deck flex as Joey walked on the area where the old man had landed. "Damn it, he broke my boat, too. Now I gotta find a new boatyard an' get it fixed."

Rut was on the bow with his cast net, motioning to Cam with a finger where to maneuver *Dancer*. His other digits, as well as his mouth, were all holding either parts of the lead-line on the skirt or bunches of net material from the twelve-foot net. Cam picked up on his subtle motions as if the pair had been netting together for years. When Rut held the finger straight up, she shifted into neutral as he twisted his body to the left then suddenly reversed direction, releasing the net from his hands and teeth in one combined motion. The centrifugal force of the lead-line caused the net to "pancake" perfectly as it settled into the water several feet out in front of the bow.

Rut watched as the lead-weighted edges sank before he started pulling on the hand-line. He could already see the silver flashes from a large bunch of menhaden that were trapped in the net as the braille lines gathered and bunched the lead-line together, sealing off the open bottom. When he got the net to the boat, he found it was filled with three- and four-inch menhaden, and weighed over twenty pounds more than when he'd tossed it. As he brought it over the gunwale, the small fish rubbing against each other left a trail of tiny iridescent scales in the water, and also on the covering board and deck of his boat. Dropping the lead-line into the baitwell he raised the horn, a small, round, open collar that the top of the net was attached to. This allowed the braille lines to slip back through it, opening the bottom of the net. He slowly withdrew the net, and prepared to repeat the process. This time after the next throw, the well was completely filled with several hundred of the frisky little baits.

"Well, that didn't take as long as I thought it might," Rut said.

"Two casts! Nice going."

"Yeah, I love it when the fish gods take pity on me," he grinned. "Let's see if they're still feeling charitable and generous."

Cam looked at him questioningly, "What do you have in mind?"

He smiled, "You'll see."

Half an hour later he directed her over toward the northernmost rip-rap edged island of the CBBT. He took one of the two pre-rigged rods down from their holders on the back edge of the tee top and freed the hook from the rod guide. He took a small dip net and scooped out several menhaden from the baitwell, chopping them into pieces on a portable cutting table that was mounted in a rod holder on the covering board. Next, he hooked a large piece of the middle section of a menhaden. He turned and looked at Cam, "Get us a little closer." When she got *Dancer* in position, he took several pieces from the table and started tossing them overboard. Then he cast his line in the middle of the chunks of chum.

"What are we after?" Cam asked.

"Cobia." He looked at her and raised one of his eyebrows. "You're not the only one with fishing intel, you know."

"Look!" She pointed back into the water where something big rolled through the chum chunks. Normally bottom feeders, cobia are opportunists and will take a meal wherever it's offered when they see it. The water was just clear enough for them to see the chum hitting the surface from down where they were.

"Here!" Rut held his rod out for her, then took the other one down from the tee top and baited its hook. As soon as his bait hit the water, it was swallowed by a nice-sized cobia.

Cam frowned, "Oh, sure, give me the rod that has all the bad luck... whoa!" A huge cobia had grabbed her bait and was already stripping line off her reel.

"You were saying?" Rut grinned. Five minutes later he brought his over the side, two inches over the minimum forty-inch size. Then he concentrated on getting the boat out in front of Cam's fish, which was putting up quite a fight. Twenty minutes later, he used a lip gaff and a gloved hand in its gills to haul her sixty-inch, fifty-eight-pound cobia on board.

"That's a beast! Wow! Thank you, Rut!"

"What for?" he asked. "You caught it."

"You got me out here."

"Thanks for the company. I might not have been tempted to go without you."

Cam looked at the two cobia that were now in the fish box. "Hey, should we go drop off the big one over at *C2* for tomorrow night's dinner? That other one is more than enough for the two of us tonight."

"Not a bad idea. And by the way, thanks for not calling my fish 'the small one.'" He winked at her.

"Why, Rut, I'd never say that! I might *think* it, but I'd never *say* it." Her eyes twinkled as she chuckled. "But that's the biggest cobia I've ever caught."

"It beat my best, too. Nice catch."

She joined him on the lean seat, putting an arm around him, "Yeah, you sure are."

∼

FRANKIE HICKS HAD BEEN UP on the second floor of Casey's tiki tower at *C2* since early in the morning. He'd already found that Shaw liked working by the pool quite a bit, and he could spread the fronds covering the side of the tower just enough to hear and see out without being seen. With only a few days remaining before they had to grab him, Mango wanted Frankie to stick close by and see if he could hear anything about Shaw's schedule. That was fine for Mango to say, since he wasn't the one who'd needed to take a leak for the past hour. Frankie had found that Shaw usually went home to his boat in time for his cocktail hour, which started over an hour ago, or he hung out here to meet up with some friends to have drinks on the pool deck. Unfortunately for Frankie, it looked like today was going to be one of those days, and he'd have to wait another couple of hours until dark before he'd be able to sneak down the stairs in the back. Meanwhile, he'd try to keep his mind off of anything that sounded like water running...

∼

TEN MINUTES later Rut secured *Dancer* alongside the bulkhead in front of *C2*. With a bit of effort, he hauled the bigger fish out of the box. The aft end of *Epilogue* was just visible beyond the corner of Casey's boathouse. Sandy was having a beer on the deck and called out, "Nice fish! Which one of you two caught it?"

"That would be me, Sandy! Thought we'd donate it to the cause for tomorrow's cookout." Cam was understandably proud of her catch.

"You know there's a cat tax to be paid on that, right?" KC had been sitting on the top of the sofa back and watched them pull up. As soon as he spotted Rut holding up the fish, he was off like a shot, heading for their boat.

Cam laughed, "I think there'll still be plenty for everyone."

"Nice cobia, Cammie," Casey commented as he walked up to the bulkhead.

"Thanks, Casey. We figured you might need it for the cookout," she replied.

"And hopefully we'll get some mahi tomorrow morning to add to it," Rut said as he stepped ashore with the fish.

"That would be great, since we're going to have quite a crowd. Nice to have a good spread with plenty of choices," Casey said.

Cam stepped ashore, and KC immediately rubbed along her calves. Sandy walked up and remarked, "He sure knows who the fisherman is amongst the bunch."

"Don't worry, KC, there's plenty to go around," Cam said.

"Speaking of plenty to go around, do you two have another beer?" Sandy asked.

Rut brushed by him with the fish, headed for the cleaning table. "Sorry, Sandy, we drank our last two on the way over here. We're 'fresh out' I guess you could say." He grinned as he used Sandy's favorite beer mooching term.

Sandy frowned at him, "You know, I used to like you."

Casey laughed, "There's plenty in the little refrigerator next to the grill pit."

"You, I still like, Casey!" He started in that direction, passing Rut who was manhandling the cobia up onto the cleaning table.

The table was cantilevered out over the water, allowing it to drain into the basin, the blood and cast-off pieces attracting smaller fish. Casey pointed out the drawer underneath it to Rut, who discovered a collection of knives and a sharpening steel arranged in a slotted organizer. Rut chose a pair of nylon handled knives; a seven-inch filet knife, and an eighteen-inch curved "Florida kingfish knife." He started sharpening the larger knife on the steel first.

Casey asked, "Thinking about steaking this one?"

Rut nodded. "The front two-thirds, then filleting the tail. That work for you?"

"I love grilled cobia steaks."

Once the knives were sharp, Rut removed the entrails with the smaller knife, tossing them over the side for the fish and crabs. Then he switched to the larger, heavier knife which cut right through the backbone, removing the head in one motion. After puncturing the eyes to ensure it would sink and not float back to the surface in a few days, he removed the little bit of meat left on the shoulder to pay the "cat tax," then the head went over the side as well. KC made short work of what was offered him and even rubbed against Rut's legs in appreciation.

"There may be hope for you yet, Rut." Sandy grinned.

"Yeah Sandy, your furry slice and dicer seems to be mellowing toward me."

"I will too if you remember to bring more beer next time."

"I thought you sold millions of books, Sandy? How can you always be out of beer?"

"Because he's the world's biggest mooch, that's why!" Captain Bill "Baloney" Cooper had walked up behind Sandy.

"Takes one to know one, Gilligan!"

"I told ya ta quit callin' me that, ya hack!"

Rut glanced over at Casey, who rolled his eyes and shook his head saying, "Bill, would you like a beer?"

"Well, since yer offerin' there Case, yeah, don't mind if I do." He went straight to the refrigerator, not needing to be asked twice, nor told where they were kept.

Casey pulled some zip-locking bags out of another drawer, along with a strange-looking hinged device. It resembled a panini press but was made from flat white plastic with thick sponge rubber sheets glued in place where the grills would normally be. Rut asked, "What the heck is that thing?"

Casey smiled. "It takes the place of a vacuum sealer when you use these kinds of bags." He placed two of the cobia steaks into a bag, then placed the bag on the foam, leaving the sealing part hanging out. He lowered the top lid and pressed it down as the two layers of foam pushed most of the air out of the bag without crushing the fish. Then he zipped the bag closed.

"That's slick!" Rut was impressed.

"Yeah, not quite as good as a vacuum sealer, but it gets most of the air out. Those vacuum sealers don't last long in the salt air."

They finished processing the larger cobia and Rut decided to donate one of the fillets from the smaller one as well. He grabbed it out of the fishbox and put it up on the cleaning table.

"What's this, the bait you used to catch the big one?" Sandy ribbed Rut.

"No, it's the one that's larger than yours. Where is yours, by the way?"

"Still swimming in the bay because somebody forgot to come by and pick me up."

"Maybe you should've told somebody you wanted to fish with them. How's somebody supposed to know you even fish?"

Sandy snorted, "I thought you said you read one of my books. You can't write books about fishing without wetting a line yourself you know."

"Okay, let's try this again. Hey Sandy, would you like to go fishing some time?"

"Well, since it looks like you may actually know a little something about it, sure, I'll go with you. Just make sure you bring plenty of beer. You pulled in here on 'suds fumes,' and that just won't do."

Casey nodded, impressed that Rut had won Sandy over so quickly, and even without having any beer on board. It was usually a large factor. Not to say that it was the only factor, since there had been people in his past that Sandy refused to drink beer with. But not many.

Rut filleted the smaller cobia, bagging and keeping half for himself and Cam, and giving Casey the other half, which went on ice in a cooler to be kept as fresh as possible until tomorrow.

Casey said, "Come on, let me mix you and Cammie drinks."

The three went up to the clubhouse where Casey made them cocktails. Then they sat in chairs next to the tiki tower.

"Hey, thanks, Casey," Rut said as he raised his glass. Cam then Casey joined him, tapping glasses before taking a sip.

"My pleasure, Rut. Thanks for the cobia. You didn't have to do that; you could've just shown up tomorrow."

"I was taught that you never show up to a party empty-handed. We appreciate the invitation," Rut replied.

"You two don't ever need an invitation to one of our cookouts. And any time you want to use this place, it's here for you. Dawn and I won't forget what you both did. But speaking of invitations, you're going to have a very busy day on Monday, Cam. You and Kari are taking a boat over to our property on Gwynn's Island, then on up the bay to *Herring Cove* in Maryland to look it over. It's going into foreclosure, and it might fit in well with our property portfolio.

"So, you're about to get a baptism by fire in one very long day. How about you two join Dawn and me here for drinks after work on Tuesday, then we'll go to the *Fin and Steak* for dinner. We'll want to hear what you think about your new job."

Cam looked surprised, then nervous. "Uh, thanks, Casey."

He laughed, "Relax, it's not a test, you won't be graded. We just like getting feedback from our new key people while their impressions are still fresh."

Rut said, "I may be closer to five-thirty getting here, Casey. We have a big job going overboard right before closing on Tuesday, so I can't skip out early on that customer. I want to see him leave in person, and don't want him to feel ignored."

"Attention to detail, Rut, I admire that. Dawn may be getting here about the same time; she has a late meeting scheduled over in Lynnhaven. So don't feel like you have to rush to get here. But we won't feel like we have to wait to start cocktail hour until y'all do get here." He grinned at Cam, who laughed and nodded.

"Sounds like a plan, Casey. I'll be here at five," Cammie said. Then looking at Rut she added, "We'll try not to be too many rounds ahead of you when you get here." She winked.

## 15

# A PLAN & A FIRST

Boarding the *Mangoritaville* an hour after dark at her slip in Lynnhaven, Frankie was bursting to tell Mango the good news. Then he saw the scowl on his face.

"What's up, Mango?"

"That freakin' moron Joey iced Daniels right on my boat. An' that old man broke my deck! Be careful where ya step around that back hatch."

"Oh, crap! Anybody see it happen?"

"Nah. We were tied up ta his dock, and there wasn't anybody around. I had him change the bait sign ta 'Sold Out,' and dump the old man overboard." Mango fell silent as he stared at his lieutenant, who was now deep in thought. Mango liked it when he did that; part of what he was paying him for was to think, and Frankie was good at it.

After a minute or so, Hicks looked up at Mango. "So, the place is deserted? And his boat's still there?"

"Yeah, it's there. And it ain't like anybody could stand ta keep that stinking old man company. Why?"

"Because this is perfect."

"How is your moron takin' out my bait guy an breakin' my boat 'perfect'? There ain't no other live bait operation near here, an' I don't trust Rut, so I can't go back ta his 'yard." Whenever anyone messed up, they became Hicks's guy, according to Mango.

"Because with that sign saying he's outta bait, nobody is gonna be stoppin' by ta chat with that stinky old man. And nobody'll give his boat a second glance if they see it runnin' around." He told Mango what he'd heard, and what he had in mind.

Despite all the pressure Mango was under, he smiled. Then he went over and dug into his bar for his bottle of *Gran Patrón Platinum* tequila, the most expensive liquor he had on board. Then he poured two generous shots and handed one to Frankie. He held his glass up to toast.

"Ta great work, an' a grand plan. And ta all of it comin' together." The two clinked glasses, then downed the smooth liquid. Mango was so relieved he refilled each of the glasses three more times over the next twenty minutes. By the end of the fourth shot, both men were feeling a warm glow and a bit numb from the alcohol and had started slurring their words, not that either noticed. Then Mango had a thought.

"I don't want you goin' near Shaw's place this weekend, there's too much risk ah ya gettin' caught. We know what we need ta know now, an' as long as they don' change their plans, we'll have this inna bag. Tuesday mornin' you an' Mikey an' th' moron take mah Jet Ski ta th' bait dock so's you can check out th' ol' man's boat fer gas 'n' stuff ta get it ready."

"Whut? Alla us gwan' fit on tha' thin'?"

"Gonna have tuh. Plenny ah power. You'll be fin'," Mango said, as he refilled their glasses one more time, the liquid spilling over the tops. But he didn't seem to realize it, or even mind if he did.

∽

MOST LIVEABOARDS ARE COMPLETELY ATTUNED to the noises their boats make. After all, their lives could depend on it. They subconsciously ignore the gentle whir and overboard discharge of their water-cooled air conditioners, the hum of their refrigerators and freezers, and even the creaking of their dock lines in wind. This, as well as the occasional hum of a bilge pump, their minds accept as normal. But if that pump doesn't shut itself off within a short window of time, it'll wake most boaters as if it were an air horn. However, what woke Sandy Morgan at 5 a.m. on Saturday didn't have anything to do with a pump or a compressor. He sat straight up in his bunk, awakened by a sudden, manmade sound. One made by knuckles rapping against the stern of his boat. He opened the large aft porthole next to his head, a pistol now in his hand.

"Who's there?" He peered out into the semi-darkness, spotting the outlines of two people aboard a center console.

A hushed voice replied, "Friends bringing beer, bait, and tackle."

"Rut? Is that you, you son-of-a-bit..."

"Yeah, me and Cammie's with me, too. You said you wanted an invitation to go fishing, well, here it is."

"Most sane people do that kind of thing a day or so before."

Cam said, "He's a spur of the moment kinda guy. I'm not used to it yet either. But are you coming with us or not?"

"Five minutes." He was actually boarding *Wave Dancer* in four. Rut slowly backed away from *Epilogue* and turned toward the basin's inlet.

"Have you had breakfast yet?"

"Funny gal. Hell no, I haven't had breakfast yet, I barely had time to hit the head. Five o'clock with no advance warning..."

Cam interrupted him sweetly, "I figured you hadn't, so I brought you some coffee and an egg-n-cheese burrito for the ride."

Sandy accepted the offerings, then sat on the bench seat in front of the console to eat the sandwich and drain the offered thermos. He'd no sooner sat down when Rut advanced the throttles, bringing *Dancer* up to her cruising speed as they passed by *Mallard Cove*'s breakwater.

Curving out and away from Fisherman Island then setting a course just off Smith Island, they raced east toward the false dawn which was about to become real. Sandy finished his breakfast then joined the pair behind the console a few minutes later, first looking aft as they sped away from land. In the distance and the now pale early morning light he could see the Cape Charles lighthouse on Smith Island, although by now he could no longer spot the land it was built on. At 191 feet, it was the tallest lighthouse in Virginia, though it had been decommissioned back in 2019. As Sandy turned and now looked out past the bow, he saw the Atlantic was about as flat as it gets, without a breath of air stirring.

"No wind, so the weed won't be getting pushed together," Sandy said.

Cam replied, "The lines were supposed to have been pretty wide yesterday, so let's hope the currents didn't break them up and they stayed together overnight. But there's always something floating."

Sandy nodded his agreement. Mahi love congregating in the shade of floating debris, and hunting under weed lines or patches, especially sargassum weed. Sargassum is a brownish algae-grass comprised of numerous leaves, stems, and tiny round air sacs that keep it buoyant. Small pieces and rafts of the weed constantly break away from the Sargasso Sea, a massive raft east of Bermuda about a thousand miles wide by three thousand miles long. Propelled by the wind, they often meet up with other rafts, forming long lines that can vary in both width and length, but are oriented in a north-south direction because of the prevailing winds. These lines can be found at different times of the year from the Gulf of Mexico up to as far north as New Jersey.

These rafts and lines are teeming with life; they're floating estuaries for everything from juvenile snails, crabs, and fish, making them the smorgasbord of the Atlantic for larger predators. Turtles, tuna, mahi, and a variety of other gamefish can often be found cruising under and around them, looking for an easy meal. Sandy recalled that as a boy growing up in the Florida Keys, he'd often shake the seaweed to see what was living in and around it. Miniature billfish, mahi, and other gamefish often less than an inch long were common finds. All were fair game to their larger cousins at feeding time.

Rut brought the boat back down to a slow cruise, waiting for the sun to get higher in the sky before they got too near the weed. Headed into the sun as they were now, it would be hard to see a weed line before they were almost on top of it, and really hard to tell if anyone was "home" underneath it. About fifteen minutes later and a dozen miles offshore they managed to spot the first of the lines. Rut turned and paralleled the line, about ten yards off, and then put the motors in neutral. But the sun was still at too low of an angle to be able to see clearly under the weed, though they thought there appeared to be some shadows darting around in the darkness underneath it.

"Okay, let's see if anybody's home," Rut said. "With as much bait as we've got, we can afford to chum a bit."

He used the dip net to scoop up a few menhaden, then tossed them out in the open water behind the boat. They immediately made a dash for the safety of the sargassum, all but guaranteeing the presence of predators. Cam was the first one with a line in the water, having hooked her menhaden through the shoulder. As Rut and Sandy baited their rods, her bait took off just under the surface. A frothy explosion happened behind the bait, an ominous spear over a foot long breaking and slashing the surface.

Rut immediately recognized it as a billfish, and yelled, "Give it line! Drop back!" But Cam had already begun doing exactly that. Suddenly the line started streaming off her spinning reel and she closed the bail, taking up the slack. Rut reminded her, "That's a circle hook, so don't 'set' it. Just keep it tight."

"I know! I've got this!"

The line was now screaming off the reel as if there were no drag at all. Then about thirty yards behind the boat a large sailfish started a series of continuous, spectacular leaps, "greyhounding" as it tried to free itself from whatever was restraining it. Then it disappeared under the surface, still taking line.

"Nice fish, Cammie. Don't horse her, just wear her out," Sandy coached.

"How do you know it's a her," Cam asked.

Sandy smiled. "Because I've caught and released more than a thousand sailfish over the years back in Florida. That's a big one, and sails that size are three times more likely to be female. Rut, let's get Cammie up in the bow and go after this old girl. Time to get some line back and set her free."

As Rut turned the boat in the direction of the fleeing sailfish, Sandy walked to the bow behind Cam, coaching and giving her encouragement. The fish leaped again a few times over the next five minutes, but it was clearly tiring, and the jumps weren't nearly as spectacular or heart-stopping as the first ones. Yard by yard, Cam began gaining on her. Finally, she was able to bring the exhausted fish alongside. Sandy reached down with a gloved hand and grabbed the fish by her bill, then carefully removed the hook from the corner of her mouth as she lay on her side on the surface. Cam leaned over the side next to him, admiring her catch.

Rut said, "Hey!" They both turned and looked up at him as he snapped several shots with his phone, then switched it to video to record the release. Sandy kept the fish pointing into the current Rut had created by idling *Dancer* forward, allowing the fish to rest and regain its strength before he finally let go of her bill. She rolled back upright, slowly moving her tail from side to side seemingly effortlessly as she swam back into the depths and disappeared. No-one on board said anything, just absorbing the moment.

Finally, Cam said, "That was my first sailfish. I caught a few white marlin back when my dad had a boat, but I've never seen a sail in real life before."

Sandy nodded, smiling as that realization sunk in. He'd just been a part of a milestone in her angling career, something he was now proud of as well. "Not as many of them this far north. Back in the Keys we had tons of sails, and a few blue marlin. It wasn't until I moved up here that I caught my first white. Very few of those down there."

Cam asked, "Isn't it unusual to see a sailfish this far in? I thought all the billfish stayed out by the canyons, another fifty miles out."

"I've seen solitary sails in fifteen feet of water before, and even saw one once inside the inlet in the Intracoastal in Palm Beach back forty years ago. Normally they prefer deeper water, but they'll follow the bait wherever it goes. Weed lines can be attractive to them, just like this one was to her today."

Rut said, "Okay crew, that was nice, but back to what we came out here for: mahi meat. If there was a sail under there, I guarantee there's some mahi around here somewhere. Let's get back to it."

~

RUT PULLED *Wave Dancer* up to the same spot on the bulkhead that he'd used at C2 the day before. The three of them started unloading their nice catch of mahi that consisted of a dozen "schoolies" and three big "bulls" up to thirty-five pounds.

"Wow! Nice morning offshore," Missy said. She, Eric, and Candi had flown down earlier and were staying overnight on *Lady Dawn*. She brought over a dock cart and began loading their fish in it.

"Oh, Missy, you don't have to do that," Cam started to say, but Sandy put a hand on her arm, shaking his head.

"It needs to get done, and I want to help. I wish I'd been there to help you guys bail a few of these, I love catching mahi," Missy replied.

As she pushed the now heavily laden cart over to the cleaning table, Sandy quietly told Cam, "She loves doing everything that has to do with fishing. She'll probably want to help clean the fish, and you need to let her if she does. For one thing, she can clean mahi faster and better than just about anybody else on this dock, but she also wants to prove herself to you. Just want you to know that in advance, but it's up to you if you want to let her."

Cam looked over at Rut, who shrugged his shoulders and said, "I'll wash the boat down, maybe you and she can clean the fish?"

"It's been a few years since I cleaned any fish, I'm not sure I remember how."

Sandy said, "Then I know someone who can help give you a

refresher course." He nodded toward Missy, who had indeed started cleaning their catch. "As for me, I think I'll go take a refresher course on the art of beer drinking. If y'all will excuse me..." He stepped up onto the bulkhead and headed for a cooler that was up on the pool deck.

# 16

# GOODBYES

The party seemed to keep growing. Cam thought that for someone whom Dawn described as being almost paranoid of large groups, Casey certainly had his share of friends. Most of the party attendees were connected to the waterfront and/or *Mallard Cove* in one way or another. She discovered that her new boss, Kari Denton, was from the Albury family, one of the larger local clans. Her two brothers-in-law worked on the water and were long-time acquaintances of Rut's. Kari's husband, Marlin Denton, headed up a huge foundation that promoted conservation in fishing. The foundation also owned a television production company and the cable mega-hit show, *Tuna Hunters*. Not that you could've proved it by Rut nor Cam, neither of whom had ever seen it.

At the party, Cam and Rut learned that Baloney had become the highest-paid star of that reality show, even though his real life was far more interesting and funny. His wife Betty proved to be a doll, and was the only person who could rein him in when he got out of hand, which was a regular occurrence.

Despite a now low seven-figure income combined from the show, his two charter boat fleet, as well as personal appearance fees, Baloney still insisted on smoking the cheapest cigars he could find, just not on land. Betty put her foot down about the putrid-smelling stogies; he could only light up once he was out on the water, well beyond the end of *Mallard Cove* inlet's jetties. Though that didn't keep Baloney from carrying around a few in his shirt pocket, and from keeping one in his mouth at all times except when eating or drinking. It was a mood barometer of sorts. When Baloney became irritated, the cigar would rapidly switch from one corner of his mouth to the other, seemingly all by itself.

But soon the cigars would be adding to his income, as a manufacturer had approached him about producing a line with his name as the brand. His thick New Jersey accent combined with that ever-present stogie had become his unofficial trademark, and the manufacturer had convinced him there was money to be made in branding. But what really sealed the deal was that the manufacturer had agreed to throw in dozens of boxes of samples each year. Free cigars held as much appeal to Baloney as mooched beer.

Casey and Eric had another thing in common, their friends ran the full income gamut. From their lawyer Greg Sawyer, his ex-model girlfriend Giselle Davis, to Timmy "Spuds" O'Shea who owned the trolling bait business at *Mallard Cove*, these party attendees all had one thing in common, they had interesting stories to tell. That, and the fact that none of them had big egos. So, Casey and Dawn's *C2* parties were like a good gumbo: a mixture of a lot of great ingredients that mingled well.

Cam recognized the faces of several people at the party from the *Cove Beach Bar*, but now she was starting to put some names with those faces. Looking around, she saw Rut was over on the other side of the pool from her, mediating a dispute between Baloney and Sandy. Of course, at the center of the conflict was beer.

"These get-togethers can be kind of overwhelming at first, but you'll get used to them and they'll become something you'll look forward to." Kari Denton smiled as she sidled up to her, intending on getting to know her new assistant a bit more out of the office. Kari was a beautiful woman, about ten years younger than Cam and about the same height, but with long raven black hair. She motioned to a pair of empty deck chairs, and the two sat down.

"There must be a hundred people here," Cam replied, looking around.

"Not quite, but close. All of them important to Casey and Dawn in one way or another, just like you are now."

"You're right. It is a bit overwhelming. And for the record, I've never been one to go drinking with my boss and her bosses before."

"Rule number one of *C2*, unless Casey is working from his chair here during the week, there are no bosses around, just friends and acquaintances. Relax and enjoy yourself, that's what this place is all about. Like most businesses, ours can get a bit stressful at times, and it's helpful to have this place to let off steam or just get away. And if you fit in as well as I think you will, you're going to come to look at a lot of these folks like they're family."

"And like family, we look out for each other." Cindy sat down next to Cam. "You're going to get taught about real estate by some of the best, especially this one here," she motioned toward Kari. "I remember when Casey and Dawn hired her as a receptionist. Not long after that, she helped them sell Eric his lot at *Bayside Estates*, and soon after that he bought into the company, partly because of her."

Cam was surprised. "I thought you'd been in real estate from day one, Kari."

She shook her head, "Nope. I earned my AA at the local community college, then went to work as a receptionist for a CPA. When he retired a couple of years later, I applied at *Bayside*. The Shaws saw something in me that I hadn't seen in myself, and not long after that I was in charge of new operations."

"They have an eye for talent, and they help you develop your talent to its full extent," Cindy said. "They hired me to run *Bayside Resort*, and the next thing I knew I was also running our new club, as well as the *Mallard Cove Hotel*, and laying out our new hotels at Lynnhaven and Cape Charles. Plus, Kari and I are working closely together on our Gwynn's Island property renovations. And Monday you guys will get the first look of any of us at *Herring Cove*. If you like what you see overall from an operations standpoint, then I'll come over to look into the hospitality side of things. You're about to get a crash course, Cam. But you'll be working under one of the best, who was taught by the best." She smiled at Kari.

"I see you've already been adopted," Rikki said to Cam as she sat down next to Cindy, handing her a glass of wine.

"It kind of feels that way, though I'm still nervous because I don't know the first thing about real estate," Cam replied.

Rik shook her head slightly, "If you did, they probably wouldn't have hired you. Then they would've had to get you to break your bad habits that you learned elsewhere. Now you'll get taught their way from the start, the same way they taught Kari. You see, they aren't just good at spotting great undervalued properties, they're also great at finding people with potential, which they've obviously seen in you. And it isn't only because you saved Dawn. So don't worry, they won't let you drown, just like you didn't let her drown, either." She smiled and winked at her reassuringly.

A COUPLE of hours and a pile of food later, Cam and Rut were talking with Rikki and Cindy when his phone rang. Excusing himself, he stepped away to take the call. Cindy said, "Once you own your own business or become part of management, that happens. This one here gets calls at all hours, but it's just part of our life." She patted Rik on her shoulder.

"Oh, like you don't? And it's not like you'll be getting less of those midnight calls when all the new properties open," Rikki retorted.

"It's still kind of surreal. Not just the job, but all of this," Cam swept her hand around the deck and pool, now lit by underwater lights and propane tiki torches.

Cindy nodded. "But it's part of why we don't mind the after-hours interruptions."

Rut rejoined the trio, visibly shaken. Cam asked, "Who was on the phone? What's wrong?"

"It was Rev. A waterman found Daniels's body in New Inlet, pretty badly chewed up by sharks, but enough of it left to identify him. He must've fallen off his dock, hit his head, and drowned."

"Oh, Rut, I'm so sorry." Cam put a hand on his arm.

"Yeah, me too. But he lived on his own terms, and died in a place he loved."

Seeing the questioning looks on Rik and Cindy's faces, Cam gave them an abbreviated version of what Rut had told her about his life and mentioned that he'd prevented the burglary at his place, without mentioning any potential Mango connections. She could see something wasn't sitting well with Rik.

"What is it, Rikki?"

Rik thought a minute then said, "It's just that I've never been much of a believer in coincidences. He spots a guy breaking into Rut's when you're in there by yourself changing, and he runs him off. Then a few days later he falls off his dock and drowns, apparently without any witnesses. It's just a little too clean for me."

Then Cam remembered the second break-in and started to say something, but caught herself, not wanting to have to tiptoe around what he might have been after.

Rik saw her hesitation. "What?"

Cam shook her head. "Nothing." She felt Rik's ice blue eyes focus on hers, and knew she wasn't buying it. But she also knew she wouldn't press the issue right then. Looking at Rut, she knew his night was ruined at the loss of his friend. She said, "We'd better go, I don't feel very festive anymore."

He nodded. "Me either. Ladies, it was nice to get to know you. I'm sorry to leave under these..."

Cindy interrupted him, "Don't be silly, we totally get it. Our condolences for your loss."

After Cam and Rut went to say goodbye to Casey and Dawn, Cindy turned to Rikki, "You think that was the whole story?"

"Hell no. He said it was Rev that called him, right? I think I may have a chat with him tomorrow after he's through with his church services. There's more to this story, and I want to find out what it is."

∼

THE NEXT AFTERNOON Rikki sat down with Reverend Eddie "Rev" Jones on the deck next to his trailer home that served as the parsonage behind the *Waterman's Church of ESVA,* where he served as the minister. "Rev, thanks for seeing me on such short notice."

Rev raised an eyebrow. "Since when are we so formal, Rik? Uh-oh, I'm getting the sense this isn't a social call. Is this about someone we have in common, or a member of my flock, or both? And how much trouble are they in?" Rev was a part of the *Mallard Cove* regulars and a close fishing pal of Murph's. He and Rik had known each other for over a year, and each considered the other a friend.

"No, it's not, I'm not sure, and again I'm not sure. Please tell me what you can about Rut Rutledge and Cammie Pinder." She watched his face closely as eyes narrowed and his forehead furrowed slightly. That "tell" let her know that he cared for at least one of them, and also might be protective of one or both.

"Rut's one of my oldest friends, and Cammie is a new friend. I'm glad that they've gotten together because they seem to be good for each other. I haven't seen Rut this happy since way before his divorce. Why are you asking, and what or who are you specifically concerned about?"

Rik repeated last night's conversation, and related her concerns. Rev knew all about both the attempted break-in as well as the successful one. Rut had kept him apprised of the situation, since Rev was the one holding the "insurance policy" which was stored on a thumb drive. He sighed as he leaned back in his chair, choosing his words carefully.

"I don't know Cammie that well, but what I do know, I like. Unless my character judgment is suddenly very flawed, I think she'll be a great addition for the Shaws, both business-wise as well as in their circle of friends. And like I said, Rut is one of my oldest friends."

Bingo, she thought. He punted when it came to Rut. "Is he involved in anything illegal? Like drugs?"

"Drugs? Sean Rutledge? Not in a million years. He wouldn't even try grass back in high school."

"Something else then?"

He sighed again. "The only thing I know going forward that he might involve himself in is maybe some numbers juggling on his 'hobby boat sales' to avoid some of both sales and personal property taxes."

"Going forward. What about in the past?"

"Rik, there are things in your past that I'd never tell another soul about. Because you're a good person, and I'd trust you with my life. Just like I would Sean."

"You mean Rut."

"One and the same person. Sean is his first name, and he's very similar to you. By that I mean he's fiercely loyal and has a good sense of right and wrong. Except when it comes to taxation."

Rik laughed. "That's okay, I'm not a tax fan either. But has he always had that good sense of right and wrong? Has he ever been violent?"

"He's never instigated violence. But he's not one to walk away from a fight if somebody picks one with him. I used to start fights at the drop of a hat when I was younger and working on the water. Never fought with Rut, but I sure did with plenty of others. I finally came around to his way of thinking when I heard my true calling and came to the church. I learned that reasoning works better than brawling, something that he'd kept telling me over the years."

"You didn't answer my question. Has he always known the difference between right and wrong?"

Rev closed his eyes and grimaced, slightly. He opened them again and stared straight into hers, "Divorce and potential financial ruin can make people do desperate things they wouldn't otherwise consider. The stronger ones can find their way back again. The smart ones make certain the past shouldn't come back to bite them in the butt."

"And Rut is...?"

"Strong and smart. As well as someone I want on my side in the game of life. In fact, he'd be my first pick when we choose teams. And you'd be my second, only because I've known him longer."

She smiled, greatly appreciating what he'd told her while staying loyal to his old friend, and yet helping his newer one. She might not know everything, but at least now she thought she might just know enough. Maybe Daniels's death was just a coincidence after all. At least she hoped it was, though something about it was still nagging at her. She'd keep her guard up and her ears open, but now she found herself wanting to trust Rut as much as Rev did.

~

SUNDAY AFTERNOON CAM pulled the throttles back and idled *Wave Dancer* up to Daniels's breakwater. Rut tied them alongside and they both climbed up on it. He hoped they might discover where Daniels went into the water; maybe find a snagged bit of cloth, or blood, some kind of sign. But what he really wanted was closure; to be able to say goodbye and let go of a man he had considered a friend. They found his skiff moored in its mostly enclosed slip, and again, there was no sign of any accident around it.

The door that led from the slip area into the two-story wood and corrugated steel living quarters was padlocked. The gas cans Big Jim filled the other day were lined up in a row, sitting on the covered dock just beyond the door, right where the old man had unloaded them. It felt like Daniels was still here, like he had just taken a trip and was planning on coming back. But in his heart and mind, Rut knew better. Knowing was one thing, but accepting was a whole different subject.

Cam slid her hand in his, giving it a slight squeeze. As bad as she felt about losing the man who had saved her from being attacked by the burglar, she knew Rut's sense of loss was huge. He'd listened to the man's stories for over a decade, and learned so much from someone who knew these waters better than anyone else around. She'd found Rut staring at Daniels's car this morning. Not like it was in the way, or like he was wondering how to go about having it hauled out of his boatyard, but as the reminder of the very unique man who had driven it and had brushed it with a fresh coat of white boat enamel every year.

She wasn't about to push him. There was the one final thing they needed to do, but only after Rut was ready to start down the road to acceptance of his loss. Then the biting flies and mosquitoes started to make their presence known, as if on cue.

Rut took it as a sign and said aloud, "Okay, Daniels, we get it." He looked at her, "Time to go."

When they reached *Dancer*, Cam stepped down into the boat and retrieved what they had brought. She climbed back up with Rut and together they made their way out to the end of the breakwater by the "Sold Out" sign. She handed him the wreath of flowers she'd woven together that morning.

"Goodbye, old friend." With that, Rut tossed the wreath off the end and watched it settle onto the water. "Let's go home, Cam."

## 17

# WORSE THINGS

On Monday Cam and Kari left out of *Mallard Cove* in the company's center console outboard. With all of their Virginia properties located on the water, the most direct way to reach them was via either the Chesapeake or the Virginia Inside Passage, so Kari had purchased this boat as a time saver the prior year. It allowed them to avoid the traffic snarls around the larger towns on their land routes, and it cut their return travel time from *Herring Cove* by more than two-thirds.

As tiring as a day running for several hours in the slight chop of the bay can be, Cam was still energized when they tied back up at *Mallard Cove*. Her first day on the job had been an exciting one. Not only had she learned a lot, but she felt like she'd made some good observations and comments that validated her being there. Best of all, she really liked working with Kari.

She didn't see Rut on the porch when she drove up, even though the 'yard was closed for the day and it was well after "beer-thirty." Walking into the house, she saw the small dining table all decked out with a linen tablecloth, cutlery, plates, candles, and wine glasses. Rut had his back to her, working on something at the kitchen counter. It turned out to be a chilled bottle of white wine; he was removing the cork after having seen her drive up.

"What's all this?" she asked. "Wine and not beer?"

As he poured two glasses he replied, "It's not every day that you get to start a new, life-changing job. I thought we'd celebrate, if that's okay."

"It's more than okay, it's thoughtful and sweet." She took a sip of wine and then looked over the top of her glass as she said, "A girl could really fall for a guy who's both of those things."

He shrugged, "Worse things could happen, I guess." He smiled as he turned back to the counter, and that's when she saw the pre-seasoned steaks, foil-wrapped potatoes, and a large bowl of salad all sitting there.

"Hey, salad! I thought you said you never fixed anything that wasn't done on the grill."

"I think I said I never *cooked* anything that wasn't done on the grill."

She set her wine down then went over and hugged Rut from behind, kissing his neck as she did.

"You keep doing that, and dinner's going to be late."

She smiled and said softly, "Worse things could happen, I guess."

∽

MANGO LOADED the last of his supplies onto *Mangoritaville*. He now had enough food on board to last him a month and a half. The only other things he'd need would be fuel and water, and those he'd have to pick up along the way though he'd topped off all the tanks today. Of course, none of this would be needed unless things went south tomorrow. Hopefully, in twenty-four hours he'd have Rut's "insurance policy" in hand, and Rut would be dead. Then the next day the redhead should be able to keep the grand jury from indicting him. While she couldn't do it all by herself, if there was one thing he knew about redheads that looked as good as she did, they could make men do just about anything they wanted. Hopefully, there would be a bunch of men on that jury or even a woman or two that liked redheaded women; it didn't matter to him so long as Shaw's wife could deliver. And from what Frankie had overheard, she was one smart, strong babe, and he was sure she would get her way. His way.

He felt the boat rock as someone climbed aboard. It was already dark outside, so with the interior salon lights on he couldn't see through the tinted windows in the aft bulkhead. He pulled his Glock from the holster in the small of his back and watched as the bulkhead door swung open. Frankie came in with a large rolled up bundle.

"What the hell, Frankie! I almost shot your ass!"

Frankie's eyes grew wide as he realized that he had come within seconds of dying. It was then that he realized how deep Mango's paranoia had become; he wasn't handling the pressure well at all. "Mango, take it easy! We got this. Two nights from tonight you'll be in the clear, an' I'll have tied up all ah the loose ends. Don't worry."

"Don't worry, you say. Yeah, I'm only facin' twenny years ta life, what's ta get upset about. Whatta you taking zen lessons from that moron Joey now?"

"Don't forget, it's my neck too, Mango. Trust me, I'll get this done."

Mango pointed to the coffee table. "Let's see whatcha got."

Frankie unrolled the vinyl lettering with the solid background that would cover over *Mangoritaville* and the mango that currently was on the transom.

"What the hell, Frankie? Are you kiddin' me? You couldn't come up with a better name than that? It sounds like a floatin' whorehouse!"

In black letters on the white solid background read "*The Happy Hooker.*"

Frankie shrugged, "Ya know, on some weekends that'd fit."

In spite of himself, Mango started chuckling. "Yeah, I guess it would. An' I guess you do see that on a lotta boats. Okay, it ain't so bad. An' I got you somethin'. A pair ah somethin's." He pointed to a box on the counter.

Frankie opened the box, which contained two yellow taser guns.

He picked one up and read the label. "Fifty thousand volts! An' three point six milliamps! Those'll melt their fillings."

"Yeah, and scramble their brains. You'll be lucky if they don't pee themselves. But they can still yell, so be sure'n get the duct tape on their mouths real quick. An' did you get that other thing?"

Frankie nodded. "30.06 Remington 700 with a scope that'll let Mikey geld a fly at five hundred yards."

"Yeah, well, he better not just geld Rut. Tell him to let him get close, then make sure he don' miss."

"Got it inna bag, Mango."

∼

T UESDAY @ *4:55 p.m.*

C ASEY HEARD the commercial boat's outboard missing terribly. One of the men in the back had the engine's cowl off of it, and the other steered it toward shore and Casey's seaplane ramp. It shut off completely right before it reached the concrete, and made a terrible grinding noise as the fiberglass bow coasted up the ramp about a foot before coming to a stop. Casey wandered over to see if he could help, but as he reached the bow the man at the helm suddenly raised a taser, and Casey's world went fuzzy as he lost control of his muscles and fell forward over the rub rail. Before he could fully regain his senses, he was trussed up and gagged with duct tape.

A WHILE later Cammie arrived at C2 expecting to find Casey, but the place looked deserted. She saw a boat pulled up at the seaplane ramp, but she didn't see anyone near it. That's when the two men who had been hiding behind the outdoor kitchen's countertop stood up and ran around it after her. She made a beeline for the fish cleaning table, intending on getting the kingfish knife out of the drawer, but she never made it that far. The shock from the taser hit her like a baseball bat, and she crumpled face-first into the concrete deck. Blood poured from her nose as the two men quickly bound her like they had Casey. The taller one threw her over his shoulder in a fireman's carry, and they hurried back to the boat, dumping her on the deck on the opposite side of the console as Casey.

As the taller one went back to the engine to reattach the spark plug wire he'd pulled and to replace the engine cover, the shorter man bent down and leered in her face. "I can't wait ta get you alone. You an' me got some unfinished business, thanks to that old man. But I made sure he won't ever get in the way again." Joey fully expected to see panic and fear on her face, but instead what he saw surprised him. There was no mistaking her look of pure, murderous fury.

~

Rut headed for New Inlet, and an outside run down to *Casey's Cove*. As he came in sight of Daniels's place, he saw that the skiff was missing. He thought to himself that it sure hadn't taken the state long to start clearing the place out. This was fast, especially for them. He ran out the choppy inlet then throttled up to fast cruising speed because the ocean was almost as flat as glass near the shore, away from the swift current of the inlet. He turned right, paralleling the coast a couple of hundred yards offshore, then hopped up on the lean seat to relax for the short, smooth run.

Pulling into *Casey's Cove* twenty minutes later, he thought it was strange that neither Casey nor Cam were there to greet him. He tied up by the fish cleaning table and climbed up onto the concrete. He was surprised to see a small pool of blood on the deck, and a trail of drops leading over toward the helipad. Using the hose from the cleaning table he washed away the blood which had barely started to dry.

"Where's Casey and Cam?" Dawn had walked up behind him.

"Oh hey, Dawn, I have no idea. I just pulled up and there wasn't anyone around, but there was a little pool of blood and a trail that went that way." He motioned toward the pad. "I'm guessing that maybe somebody cut their hand cleaning fish, and they're off bandaging it somewhere?"

Dawn looked concerned as soon as she heard about the blood. She shook her head, saying, "The first-aid kit is in the clubhouse. There's nothing like that over by the helipad."

She pulled her phone out of her purse and called Casey. They heard his phone ring somewhere beyond the helipad. Looking at each other, the two of them then rushed toward the sound. Rut called Cam's phone and again they heard ringing coming from the same direction. Now racing across the helipad, they discovered both phones in the marsh grass right at the edge of the seaplane ramp. Curiously, there was another phone next to them, one of the prepaid kind you can get in a convenience store. A note addressed to Rut was attached to it with a rubber band: "*Rut, hit speed dial #1 when you and Red are together. I don't wanna have to repeat myself.*"

"What the hell is that about?" Dawn exclaimed.

Rut looked confused, then dialed the number and put it on speaker. Mango answered.

"Well, I guess you two already figured I got Shaw and your girl, Rut. Kinda funny, 'cause it's gonna take two different things if you wanna get 'em both back. First, Red, if you wanna see your hubby again in one piece, you're gonna do me a favor. One ah the cases you'll hear tomorra on that grand jury is mine. Rut'll fill ya in on me. You're gonna tank that indictment, or I'll send your guy back, one piece at a time. This ain't no joke; Rut'll tell you that. You got what I'm sayin'?"

Dawn said, "Who are you? What do you mean? How can I stop an indictment? Where's Casey? Is he alright?"

"He's fine, for now. I tol' ya, Rut'll fill you in on me, and as long as I get what I want, you'll get what you want, your old man back. See, tomorra that new grand jury'll get organized, and first thing they'll do is elect a foreman. You make sure you get elected, then you can run the show, and steer 'em all away from indictin' me. All you hafta do is make sure the US Attorney don't get twelve votes to indict. It's not like you gotta convince everybody. Pick out the weak ones and pressure 'em."

"What if I can't?"

"Oh, I think you can. I know that you damn sure better. Act like your hubby's life depends on it, 'cause it does. Again, Rut'll tell you I ain't playin' around."

"How do I know Casey's not hurt? There's blood on the ground. Let me talk to him."

"He's not with me right now, but he's fine. The boys said the girl took a header and busted up her nose, but they're both okay."

Rut spoke up, "You better not hurt Cammie!"

"Rut, you know better than ta try ta threaten me. An' you know I'm a businessman; hurtin' her or him would be bad business. I'll only do that if I don' get what I want, 'cause that'd be good business."

"What do you want from me?" Rut asked.

"You know what I want. That 'insurance policy.' An' I want all the copies."

Rut looked down, unable now to look at Dawn. What he saw on the concrete ramp made his heart skip a beat. "All right, Mango." He sighed, "There's only one thumb drive."

"Ya know what? I believe you, Rut. You've always been too honest fer your own good, an' you've never lied ta me. So, here's what you're gonna do. You're gonna go get it, and then take it to the Cape Charles lighthouse over on Smith Island in two hours. I guess I don't need ta tell you to come by yourself, and not ta call the cops or I'll know, an' you'll never see your little chicky again, at least not in one piece. An' you know better than ta think I'm bluffin'. I knew about my case comin' up in front ah the grand jury, an' about Red bein' on it. Trust me, either of ya call the cops, I'll know it. An' then there won't be enough glue in Virginia ta put your little chicky and Shaw back together again. Two hours, Rut. Don't be late." The call ended.

Dawn grabbed Rut by his upper arms and shook him. She was totally furious, believing that Rut had sold them out. She yelled in his face, "What have you done? Who is this guy, and how the hell do you know him?"

"He's a criminal from over in Virginia Beach. He's into loan sharking, selling hot boat gear, and I don't even know what all else."

She shook him again, "Why are you two on a first-name basis?"

He looked down again. "I borrowed money from him after my divorce so I could save my business. It's a long story, but I ended up in the hot boat gear part with him for a while, paid him back, then got out of the business."

"And Cammie told you about me being on the grand jury, and then you told him. You're a damn criminal!"

"Cammie would have never done that. I'd have never done that, either. You told him yourself! We were at the table next to you and Lindsay when you read your letter, and we overheard you. But I have no idea how he knows what's coming before the grand jury. People say he's got connections, I just don't know who or where. But I think I know where he's taken Cam and Casey." He pointed to two identical purple marks on the seaplane ramp, about seven feet apart. "I know the boat that made those marks. I helped my friend Daniels paint the bottom of his boat, and it's the only one I've ever seen with that color of bottom paint. He mixed it himself. I know where it docks, which is the same place Daniels died on Saturday. Now I don't believe that was due to natural causes like they said.

"I'm thinking his place on Godwin Island might not be vacant now. The boat was missing when I came out the inlet on the way here. See how those narrow marks are parallel? It's part of why I'm sure they used his boat. Those are from the reverse chines that stick down under a flat-bottomed *Carolina Skiff*'s bow. See how dark they are going straight in, but then in reverse they lighten up as they curve to the south? That's when they were backing up, and the paint was wearing through to the fiberglass on the rough concrete. And it means the bow was pointing north when they left, up the Virginia Inside Passage. Which explains why I didn't run into them on the way down here. They came down on the inside route, while I went out in the ocean."

Dawn said, "If you know where they are, then let's go bring them home."

"You're not going anywhere."

"Who the hell are you to tell me anything? It's all because of you they got taken! You brought this to my door..."

"You're right, and you have no idea how sorry I am about that. But if you go with me and something goes wrong, they're both dead. But if that happens with just me, you still can free Casey and maybe Cam too by doing what Mango wants."

Dawn started dialing her phone.

"What are you doing! He said no cops!"

"I'm not calling the cops; I'm going to get Rikki to go."

"I'm not taking anybody else with me, Dawn."

"You're right; she's taking you with her. She'll be the one in charge."

"What makes you think I would agree to that?"

"Have you ever killed a man, Rut?"

"No."

"That's why. She's killed plenty. And after we get Casey and Cam back, you stay the hell away from here. I never want to see you again.

## 18

# PAYBACKS

Rut figured that Mango wouldn't know he had come down by boat. Since they had apparently used the Inside Passage route to go up to Godwin Island, if in fact they *were* on Godwin Island, he decided to retrace his steps and run back in the ocean. He'd begrudgingly agreed to Rikki going along with him, and he was meeting her at his boatyard. A plan had begun to take shape in his head, and if she was as good and as experienced as Dawn said, he wanted to run it by her. Especially since she was going to play a big part in it.

Running back in New Inlet, he glanced back at Daniels's place and saw the skiff was back in its covered slip. He knew for certain now that he'd been right about where they had taken Casey and Cam. And they were still there, which was a good sign, or so he thought. Several minutes later he pulled into the boatyard where he spotted Rikki waiting on the dock. She started to step aboard when he pulled up, but he waved her off, grabbing a single spring line to temporarily tie up the *Scarab*.

"Come with me, I need to get something." He saw that she was dressed in dark clothing, and had some type of a tactical belt around her waist with pockets of gear.

As they hurried to his house she said, "I need to know everything."

He nodded. "I'll tell you on the way." Once in the house he grabbed the Glock from behind the bedside table, and extra rounds for the .44 magnum from his safe. Rik didn't even comment on his stacks of cash. He gave her the Cliff's Notes version of how he met Mango, what he knew of his business, and how he'd referred to "the boys" kidnapping Cam and Casey. Then he told her about both break-ins. He also told her about the marks at the seaplane ramp and seeing the skiff back in its slip. Then he explained his plan. She nodded her approval.

As they neared New Inlet, Rut pointed out that Daniels's boat was still there. Rik asked, "Do they know this boat?"

"No, it's new to me. Plus, I haven't gotten around to putting the name on her sides yet."

Rik pulled a Sig Sauer nine-millimeter from her holster, then took a silencer from another pocket on the utility belt and screwed the two together. Rut watched and looked at her quizzically.

"Don't ask, just trust me. I like your plan, but you are going to follow me," she said.

"I don't have a silencer for either of mine."

"Which may be a good thing, Rut. There are times when it helps to make noise. And there isn't a soul within a mile of that island to hear that cannon."

They pulled out of the inlet, turned right, and anchored just offshore and opposite Daniels's place. They could see the top of the roof over the dune and the scrub trees. They both silently slipped over the side into waist-deep water, making their way into the beach. Rik took point as they made their way down one of Daniels's trails that led back to his shack. The mosquitoes and biting flies were thick in the scrub, but both of them were too intent on freeing their friends to pay much attention to them. As they reached the edge of the brush, Rik held up a hand for Rut to stop.

From their position they surveilled Daniels's place, which was made up of a trio of buildings that were tied together and built out over the water on wood pilings. One of the units was two stories tall. There was an old bulkhead along the shore made from used railroad ties, and a rusty metal catwalk ran from it out over the water and to a steel door on the first floor of the two-story building. Rik motioned for Rut to watch the two windows in the second story that overlooked their position, and she started across the catwalk. Upon reaching the door Rik tried the knob and discovered it was locked. She put her ear to the door, and held up two fingers, indicating she could hear two different voices inside. The voices faded and then reappeared near the covered slip that housed the skiff. She quickly retreated back to Rut's position as they both heard the outboard crank up.

Rik whispered, "I heard two different men, and neither was Casey. I didn't hear him or Cammie."

They watched as the skiff now came into view, idling out clear of its slip. Even from the back and at this distance, Rut was pretty certain it was Mikey. He throttled up, and the skiff went out and around the point of Godwin Island, heading for the inside route down to Smith Island.

"Pretty certain that was Mikey, which just leaves Mango, Frankie, and Joey," Rut said.

"Well, we're not getting in through the front door, so maybe we can get in the back way," Rik whispered.

They both watched the upper windows as they made their way over the bulkhead into the waist-deep water. Fortunately, the *Carolina Skiff* didn't draw much, so Daniels had never bothered to dredge the slip. The water was only mid-thigh deep as they slipped under the partial wall that protected the side of the slip. There was a Wave-Runner tied up against the back dock, next to all the gas cans.

Rut saw that the hasp on the door was now broken, and hung down with the padlock still attached. He pointed to the door, and to a ladder at the back dock that went down into the water. They both climbed the ladder onto the dock and then moved over to the door. Rik opened the door as silently as possible; it led into a small kitchen. Casey was lying on the floor in a corner, still gagged and bound with duct tape. His eyes filled with relief when he recognized Rik. A quick scan of the room told her he was the only one in here. Casey was now nodding his head violently at the stairwell on the far side of the little room where two voices could be heard above. Rut tapped Rik's shoulder and motioned for her to free Casey. Then he pointed to himself, and the stairwell. Rik shook her head violently, motioning for him to wait. He shook his head and mouthed "Cam." He'd recognized her voice, and Joey's. He couldn't, and wouldn't, wait a second longer.

∾

Mikey picked up the waterproof case that held the Remington. "Remember, she's gotta stay alive until after I off Rut. Just in case things go sideways, and we need ta prove she's still breathin', you know what I mean?"

Joey nodded reluctantly. "Got it. Besides, she'd be no fun dead." He grinned cruelly.

"You're freakin' sick, you know that, Joey?"

"Says the guy who's gonna whack Rut from fifty feet up. Not even close enough ta see his face. At least that old man died lookin' at me."

"Hey! What I'm doin' is *business*! You had ta off the old guy 'cause you got sloppy, and just *had* to try getting some leg off that chick. You need ta keep your pecker in your pants and do your thinkin' with your big head from now on."

Joey replied, "I'm just mixin' a little pleasure with my business, and that's none a your business. I'll keep her alive, long enough. You just make sure you don't miss. But take your time gettin' back here, 'cause that'll be the end of my fun. Unless you wanna tag team her when you get back."

"You are a freakin' sicko. I'm a professional, I don't do rape. And I don't wanna hear any more about what you do. I'm gonna go shoot Rut, take that insurance thing over ta Mango on his boat, then I'll come back here. You better be through with whatever you're gonna do before I get back." He climbed down into the skiff, and left.

Joey walked back through the door, eyeing Casey in the corner. "Guess you heard all that, huh. You're the lucky one. When your wifey gets Mango in the clear, you get ta go home. Ain't the same for her upstairs. Well, no sense lettin' her go ta waste, huh."

Casey watched Joey disappear up the stairs, feeling the most hopeless he'd ever been in his entire life, having no way of preventing what was about to happen to Cammie. And he wasn't fooled by what Joey had said; there was no way they were going to let him out of here alive. And he knew they planned to kill Dawn, whether she was able to stop the indictment or not. He just hoped that she had called Rik, who would make sure she stayed safe.

Joey walked into Daniels's bedroom where Cammie was tied to the iron head and footboards of the old man's bed. She glared at him. He said, "Oh, look at you, still got that fire in yer eyes. I hope that ain't the only place ya got it." He went over and started unbuttoning her blouse, but stopped and laughed. "What the hell, it ain't like you'll be buttonin' it back up." He ripped the rest of her blouse open, popping a couple of the buttons. He kept watching her eyes, expecting and hoping for that fire to change to fear, but the fire only got deeper, and that unnerved him a little. Wanting to take back the control he felt slipping away, he took out his switchblade and held it in front of her face for effect as the blade sprung open. She didn't flinch, and that irritated him.

"The other day, I watched you dancin', wishin' you'd turn around for me so I could get a look at all the goods, not just your butt. Well, it looks like I'm gonna get my wish today." He slid the knife blade under the center of her bra, cutting the fabric linking the two cups. With the tip of the blade, he flipped the two cups to the sides. "Whatta we got here! Looks like somebody beat me to you." He traced the scar with the tip of the blade, expecting her to flinch. When she didn't, he realized things really weren't going the way that he wanted and expected. He didn't feel nearly the same amount of heat or excitement now that he had when he'd seen her through the window. Realizing he needed to do something to make her fully understand the situation she was in he said, "I think I'll give you a matching slice on this other one. Shame it'll never have time ta heal an' scar up." Still no reaction.

Now he was the one who was getting mad. He took the knife and cut through the tape on her mouth, then ripped it away from her face and hair. "What the hell is wrong with you, bitch? You got no idea what's about ta happen ta you."

Instead of cowering, she laughed at Joey. "Yeah, I know, it's happened before. But you don't know what's in store for you. You like this scar? I cut the whole package off the guy who did it as I watched him die, just like I'm gonna do with you."

Now Joey's fury was ramping up, he lay the knife on the mattress and in one violent motion he yanked down her pants and panties. "I don't think so, bitch. My package is gonna be a little too busy." He unbuckled his belt and dropped his pants to the floor. Then he bent over to drop his shorts. As he straightened back up, he grabbed his knife right before he heard an unmistakable sound behind him; it was the sound of a Smith & Wesson revolver being cocked. He spun partly around, legs still tangled in his pants and shorts just as Rut fired the first shot. It caught him in the shoulder of the hand that held the knife, a non-fatal shot that knocked him back against the bed as the knife fell from his grasp. Being a dual-action revolver, there was no need for Rut to cock it again since it fired when he pulled the trigger a second time. That second bullet passed through Joey's abdomen, the specialized defensive round mushrooming before it tore out a chunk of his spine about an inch and a half in diameter when it exited, rendering everything below his diaphragm numb. He fell back across Cam's legs like a sack of potatoes.

Cam said to Rut, "Untie me!"

Rut picked up Joey's knife and sliced through the rope binding Cam's feet and hands. She kicked Joey off her legs, then pulled up her panties and pants. She removed the wrecked bra then closed her shirt with the few remaining buttons. Cammie took the knife out of Rut's hand then said, "Go downstairs, I'll meet you there."

He suddenly realized what she intended on doing. "Cam, he's going to die anyway."

She turned and glared at Rut. "This isn't about him, this is about me, and it's *for* me. Now *GO!*"

Rut hesitantly turned and went down the stairs. Cam climbed

onto the bed where Joey lay on his back, moaning. He looked into her eyes, seeing satisfaction slowly replace the fury in hers as terror crept into his own. She smiled as she said, "I told you what would happen to you. I'm just sorry you can't feel it now."

Two minutes later Cam came down the stairs with a bloody mass in her hands. Walking out the door to the boat shed she threw it into the middle of the empty slip, where it slowly sank. She went into the kitchen to wash the blood off her hands in the shack's only sink. Then she scrubbed off the caked blood and rinsed the scratches on her face that she'd gotten in the fall when she was tazed. Rut, Casey, and Rik watched her silently. She and Rik locked eyes, and after a long pause Rik nodded slightly in agreement with what she'd done to Joey.

Rut said, "We need to torch this place. Too much DNA, too many questions, not enough good answers. Not to mention, the body. The state would eventually demolish the place anyway, so we'll be saving the taxpayers some money."

Cam asked, "What if Mango sees what happened to it?"

Rut shook his head, "Mango isn't coming near this place again. Mikey took off in the skiff..."

Casey interrupted, "He's going to your meeting place, and he said he's going to shoot you from fifty feet up, then take some insurance thing to Mango on his boat."

"That all makes sense. The meeting is at the Cape Charles lighthouse on Smith Island. I'll make sure he won't be coming back. Frankie Hicks is too smart to be seen around here, and Mango gets him to direct all the rough stuff. He'll keep Frankie close to him, just in case."

Cam told him, "You're not going to that meet!"

"Oh, yeah I am, and then I'm going after Mango. If it wasn't for me getting involved with him in the first place, none of this would've happened to you guys. We wouldn't have had lunch that day, and he wouldn't know Dawn is going to be on the grand jury. And Rikki wouldn't have had to risk her life to save y'all. No, this is my mess, and I'm going to be the one to go clean it up."

"Then I'm going with you," Cam said.

"The hell you are."

"The hell I'm not!" Cam fumed. "Like you said, this all happened because of things you did. I just relived my nightmare all over again because of it. So you don't get to tell me what I can and can't do."

Rik put a hand on her arm. "He's right, Cam, you can't go because you don't have the right training."

"He can't go alone, Rik, I'm not going to have his getting killed weighing on my conscience."

"You're right, he can't go alone." Rik looked at Rut. "That's why I'm going with him."

Rut said, "Rikki, it was one thing for you to put yourself in harm's way to save Casey and Cam. But this is about me. I can't ask you to risk your life for somebody you don't really know."

"You're right, you can't. Because you don't need to, I'm going, with or without you. Now let's take those gas cans and soak this place."

Cam was still angry but asked, "What about the WaveRunner?"

Casey, who'd been quiet up until now spoke up and said, "Leave it. Let it burn. I hate those frigging things. They scare the heck out of fish."

## 19

## HEAVY PRICE TO PAY

The ride back to the boatyard was done in silence. Cam wouldn't even look at Rut, much less talk to him, and she sat in front of the console. He wasn't certain if it was about his association with Mango that had brought all the trouble into their lives, or his refusal to take her along with Rik and him. Probably a mixture of the two things he figured, and quite likely a relationship killer. There was no getting past how he'd caused all this.

Rik had texted Dawn that they were all safe and headed back to the 'yard. Dawn then broke all the speed limits in her car getting there before they did, and was waiting on the dock for them when they pulled in. She first wrapped herself around Casey before hugging Cam and Rik as they got off the boat. She didn't go near Rut.

"I'm just glad you're all safe."

Rut knew that didn't include him.

Rik said, "Okay, you all stay here, it's safer than *Mallard Cove* right now because Mango won't think to have anyone look for you here. Rut and I will go deal with this."

"Wait, what? You're going back after them?" Dawn asked.

"You won't be safe until we get every last one of them, Dawn. That means Mango too, because you testifying against him could mean life for the guy," Rikki said. "Okay, Rut, let's go."

Right before he stepped down into the boat, Cam came over to Rut and looked him in the eyes. She hesitated a minute, possibly to choose her words carefully as well as to restrain herself. "I want you to know one thing, it was what you said that night on the porch. It was how you got me to start looking at what had happened to me and what I did, all in the right way. That's what got me through this; what kept me from letting him have any power over me. And I'm not letting anybody have power like that over me again." Her eyes bored into his right before she finished with one very cutting word, "Ever." Then she turned and walked down the dock, never looking back. Rut knew she was talking about him telling her she couldn't come with them. And he knew when he got back, she'd be gone.

"RIKKI, thanks again for going with me." They had just passed through New Inlet. From the channel they'd seen that Daniels's place had gone up like kindling, and there was only a little bit of the metal roofing material and some smoldering pilings left sticking above the surface. The rest of the building had either burned or collapsed into the water. Fortunately, in this less populated part of the world, the fire had gone unnoticed.

She glanced at him, realizing that he had the wrong impression. "You were right when you said there was no way you could ask me to go to protect somebody I'd just met. I'm not going for you, I'm only going so I can protect Casey, Dawn, and Cam. That's not a job I'd trust to anyone else, especially someone whose flawed judgment allowed him to get mixed up with these people in the first place. This is our best chance to get to them because they don't know we're coming. If I let you go by yourself and you screw it up, then it would be that much harder for me to finish the job."

Rut sighed. "Understood. Thanks for putting your cards on the table."

"You needed to know. And I need to know, is your head on straight enough for this after what happened back at the dock? I don't mean to pile on you, but I want to make sure that losing your woman isn't going to be too big a distraction."

If he'd had any doubts about what Cammie had meant, Rikki had just confirmed it. "I'm good."

She studied him for a moment, then seemed to accept his answer. "Have you ever been in that lighthouse?"

He nodded, knowing she'd want as much tactical info as possible. "You already know it's tall, the tallest in Virginia at almost two hundred feet. Built in the late 1800s, all cast iron, and the sections are bolted together. The center is a tube about twelve feet wide, and it's anchored by eight large metal pipe legs about twenty feet out from the base of the tube. They're connected by a bunch of cast iron tension rods in 'X' patterns that are about three inches in diameter. Gives the place a spiderweb look.

"Inside the tube is a spiral staircase about three feet wide on either side, with an open shaft about six feet across between them. There are four windows that look out the front, and from what Casey said, it sounds like Mikey will be at the first one, about fifty feet above the ground. That will give him a great field of fire with two exceptions. There are ten-inch pipes attached to the center tube right below the bottom window corners that run out horizontally to the legs. So long as I keep one of those legs or a horizontal brace between me and that window, it should make it next to impossible for him to get a clear shot at me.

"The best part is that Mikey shouldn't be aware we know not only that he intends on shooting me, but where he's going to shoot from. And he's not expecting anyone else to come with me, especially not someone slogging their way through the biggest, most treacherous marsh on the ocean side."

Rik nodded at Rut, impressed with his knowledge and plan. "Not to be mean, but how does somebody as smart as you seem to be, get involved with Mango and end up losing someone like Cam in the process?"

Rut paused a beat before answering, "Don't take this as an excuse, just an explanation. Have you ever gotten hooked up with the wrong... woman that you were certain was the right one? And I'm not talking about Cam in my case. Then when you got blindsided, it totally destroyed your life and your world? When that happens you can't think straight, and you do things you never in a million years thought you would do to protect what little of your former life you have left."

"Point taken."

Rut sighed. "You know the biggest difference between you and me, Rikki? When the right woman came along, you were smart enough to figure out how to keep her."

"So, were you thinking more long-term about Cam?"

"I'd kind of let myself start to think that way. More like hoped to I guess, though I hadn't even told her that yet. But with her working for the Shaws now, even if I was able to get her back, they don't want me around them again. Not something I blame them for. But with the way that group all work and play together, being with me would get Cam shut out of things and hold her back in her new career. I'm not going to do that. So, the best thing I can do for her is to let her go and not try to get her back, assuming I even come out of this in one piece. That ship has sailed, so let's not talk about it anymore, and just focus on what's ahead."

Rik silently thought over what he'd said. She hoped he could "...just focus on what's ahead." He'd need to be and stay one hundred percent focused if they both were going to get this job done and come out of it alive.

RUT DROPPED Rik off on the ocean side beach of Smith Island. He hoped that Mikey was indeed at the window that faced west, and not up in the top of the tower where he could easily spot Rik coming across the marsh. Rut knew she had a roughly half-mile slog through some of the most inhospitable environment that ESVA had to offer, with mud, marsh grass, as well as thick clouds of mosquitoes and biting flies. It was a little over an hour from sunset, meaning it was "happy hour" for anything with wings, teeth, and a thirst for blood. His trek from the water to the tower would be a fraction as long, but just as much of a nightmare. He planned on hitting the shore on the far side in sight of Mikey, right on that two-hour deadline. He wanted to give Rikki as much time as possible to get through the marsh. That meant he needed to hit the shore thirty minutes from now.

Rut turned and ran offshore for ten minutes, then reversed course, tucking in just offshore of the beach, and rounding the point at the southern tip of the island. From there he could see *Mallard Cove* off in the distance. Careful to leave some room between his boat and the stacks of underwater shellfish cages in the aquaculture farm that paralleled the shoreline, he started up a winding creek that led to one of the only dry landing spots available. That's where he spotted Daniels's skiff pulled up to the beach. He knew the long line of low trees that ran parallel to the marshy shore would give him cover until he broke out into the open, then he had to start making his way directly toward the tower. He was counting on Mikey not shooting too soon, before he got close enough to put a tower leg between the two of them.

When he broke out into the clearing, he spotted Rikki over at the tower base. She was tucked up against the tower tube, making her way around to a catwalk that was about six feet up in the air. It led from the tower entrance out beyond the perimeter of the iron spider-web, and to a set of steps that led down to the marshy ground. But where Rik was, there weren't any steps. She seemed to defy gravity as she pulled herself up onto the walkway using only her arms until she reached the top of the white-painted iron railing and was able to swing her legs over it.

Mikey had made the crucial mistake of leaving one of the two large metal doors open. Its rusty, hundred-year-old hinges would have surely squeaked in protest on being opened, announcing Rik's presence and alerting him to there being another person with Rut. But Mikey was either overconfident, stupid, or both. Rik disappeared into the tower as Rut continued making his way forward, now being careful to stay in the cover of the supports. Two minutes later the window lit up with a flash, and there was a noise like a cannon shot. Pulling out his revolver and taking no pretense of cover, Rut now raced across the soggy field to the stairs, taking them two at a time. Just as he reached the doorway, a body fell headfirst down the center shaft onto the iron floor. He didn't need to look any closer to see that Mikey was dead. A minute later, Rik came trotting down the stairs, holding a rifle, and shaking her head slightly as if to clear it.

"Damn flash-bang in a metal tube. Talk about the worst possible scenario. I was eight feet below him with my ears covered, my eyes closed, looking away and it still rang my bell. It was like standing next to a Howitzer when it fired. He was on a flat iron platform and it blew up right at his feet, so he really got the worst of it. Didn't take much after that to push him over the railing."

Rut asked, "What do we do with the body?"

"Nothing. We take his phone and ID then leave him be. We take the skiff, too. Just some poor bastard that slipped and fell over the rail. It's not like anybody else'll be coming over here until winter, after the bugs are gone. By then, he'll be a pile of bones and goo."

Rut nodded, then looked concerned. "Wait, if we take the skiff, how does it explain how he got here?"

"By the time he's found, they'll think his kayak must've floated away in a storm. They find a couple empty ones of those around here every year. Now let's go, we're not done yet and the bugs are already getting thick."

∽

EVEN USING THE BURNER PHONES, Frankie had told Mikey and Joey to keep the phone and text chatter to a minimum. But it was now 9:10 p.m. Mikey was supposed to have been at *Mangoritaville* ten minutes ago at the latest with that thumb drive.

"Call 'em, Frankie. I don't like not hearin' from them."

Frankie hit the first then the second speed dials on his burner. "No answer on either one, Mango."

"Son of a bitch! I knew your numbskulls would screw this up!"

"Wait," Frankie pointed out the salon's side window. Mango had intentionally tied up outside of the "Tee" at the end of the dock so they could watch and see any boat coming through Lynnhaven Inlet under the Lessner Bridge. "That looks like the bait guy's boat. Somethin' must've happened to Mikey's phone."

They'd drawn all the curtains in the salon except for the port side, which faced out into the channel and over to the bridge. This was the second boat they'd seen in ten minutes, but the first was an old *Scarab* they didn't recognize. As they focused out over the water, they suddenly heard the busted aft deck crunch under someone's weight. Someone who'd been very careful not to rock the boat while slowly transferring their weight onto it.

Mango killed the salon lights and hit all the cockpit floods a second before Rik burst through the door, her Sig leading the way. The blinding lights had disoriented her just enough to give Frankie the advantage in the darkened room as he grabbed the Sig's silencer, using its extra leverage against her hand while Mango pointed his pistol at her from across the cabin.

"Drop it," Mango said.

Rik relinquished her hold on the Sig and Frankie took it away from her. Then he moved in behind her in the doorway, twisting one arm behind her back. He shoved her forward and reached behind him to close the door. Then for the second time today, the cocking of Rut's .44 magnum announced his presence, and he prodded Frankie in the back with the barrel. "Drop it, and let her go," he told Frankie who hesitated until Rut prodded him again.

Mango's arm shot out and grabbed Rik, and he pulled her back against him as a shield, his gun now stuck in her side as he wrapped an arm around her neck.

"Let her go, Mango. It's over."

Mango laughed, "Over? Ya wish it was over. I'm just gettin' started with you, ya damn turncoat."

"Any minute now a team of FBI agents will be coming down the dock. It'll be best for you to let her go, and drop your gun."

"You seen too many cop shows on TV, Rutledge. If you'd gone ta the Feds, it'd be them instead ah you standin' there. An' since Joey and Mikey never made it back here, I'm guessin' you could be up for a double murder rap. So, you didn't call the Feds. But it also means you got Shaw an' your chick back, and then tomorrow I'm gettin' indicted. Time for me ta take a boat ride an' disappear. Sorry, Frankie, but I'm goin' alone." Mango took his gun out of Rik's side just long enough to shoot Frankie. Standing behind him, Rut felt a hot poker hit him in his side, and Frankie crumpled to the salon deck at his feet.

Mango said, "It was his guys that messed up, and now I just doubled how far my supplies'll go. Now toss your gun over here, on the deck."

When Rut complied, Mango shoved Rik over to him, as he bent down to pick up the big revolver. He kept his gun trained in their direction but his focus was now on the stainless pistol. Rut drew the Glock out of his back holster and began firing, his first bullet hitting Mango's gun hand, preventing him from shooting. Then he kept firing into Mango's torso until he lay prone and motionless on the deck.

Rik grabbed Rut's gun arm and pushed it down. "Whoa! You can only kill him once, Rut. Nice shot on his gun hand."

"It would've been if that's where I'd have been aiming. I was going for a head shot."

Rikki grimaced, shaking her head slightly. Then she peeked out between the curtains and down the dock. "Looks like our luck's still holding. The dock's deserted, and if there is anyone aboard any of these boats, they probably have their A/C going and their TVs on, so they didn't hear anything." She turned and looked at Rut, who was now holding his side above the belt line. Blood was seeping out between his fingers. "You're hit!"

He nodded, gritting his teeth. "Bullet went through Frankie and into me."

Rut leaned against the arm of the sofa while Rik took a knife and cut his shirt open by the wound. "Looks like it's through and through, and didn't nick anything major. But we need to stop that bleeding."

"I've got a full offshore first-aid kit on my boat in the console. Sutures, clotting sponges, the works."

"Good, because we can't take you to the hospital without the police getting involved, and we don't have any good answers as to how you got shot." Rik went to *Wave Dancer* and retrieved the kit. Then she lay Rut on his side on the couch with his shirt pulled up and hit him with the clotting sponges on both the entry and exit wounds.

"Damn it, that hurts worse than getting shot!"

"I know that from experience, too. By the way, you did good tonight. I'm glad you waited until just now to wimp out." She grinned at him. "No Novocain in the kit?"

He gritted his teeth and shook his head, knowing she was going to have to suture the wounds.

Rikki peeled back each sponge and shook antibacterial powder into the wounds, then put a few stitches in both. She finished by taping bandages over each. "Done. Now that wasn't too bad, was it?"

"I'm buying some Novocain for that kit first thing in the morning, does that answer your question?"

Rik laughed and took out her phone. She texted Cindy an "OK" before sending Dawn a "thumbs-up" emoji. Neither expected any more details via electronics where they'd leave a trail; those would have to wait until later when they were face to face. She looked at Rut, "You think you can withstand a boat ride?"

He nodded, "Whatever you need me to do. I owe you big time. Where are we going?"

She pointed offshore. "Edge of the shelf. Time for a Viking funeral. But first I need to go wipe your prints off Daniels's boat's helm. That way they'll figure some kid stole it and abandoned it here. Be right back."

## 20

# RUT'S FIGHT

It was sometime after two a.m. when they reached the edge of the shelf. Rik had run *Mangoritaville* at a slow cruise since they were having to tow *Wave Dancer* behind them. It also helped to provide a smoother ride for a wounded Rut. She checked the radar and this far out, there wasn't another boat on the screen. Rik had picked this spot because it was far enough away from the more frequently fished canyons. They wanted the deeper water, but they also didn't want *Dancer* to be seen on anyone's radar as leaving the scene when the Ocean Yacht burned, since the flames would be visible at sea for miles.

Throttling back to idle, she joined Rut down below by the head. He had been busy piling up cardboard from Mango's cases of provisions, the foam rubber from the vee berth's mattresses, sheets, paper, curtains, and anything else he found that was loose and would burn. Once this pile ignites in such a small, mostly enclosed area, it should burn hot enough to start melting the polyester resin in the fiberglass and wood bulkheads as well as the fiberglass superstructure itself. When fiberglass begins to burn, flammable chemicals separate in the resin, and the chemical fire that's created is next to impossible to extinguish without being totally immersed in water or foam. The fire should begin to spread rapidly.

Satisfied that the ignition pile was almost ready, Rik went back in the cockpit and pulled Dancer up to the transom, tying her off with a single line, about two feet from the stern. She cranked both outboards in neutral, allowing them to warm up. Then she climbed back onto *Mangoritaville* and up to the flying bridge, making sure the hydraulic steering was keeping the boat idling straight offshore. She took a small spool of eighty-pound-test monofilament line and tied it to both of the throttle levers, running the line up and around a wide conduit pipe that went up to the overhead radio box. The pipe's curved surface should work almost as good as a pulley for reversing the direction of the monofilament. Carefully she played out the spool, running the line back down to *Wave Dancer,* and securing it to the starboard spring cleat.

Rut came out of the salon after glancing back at the bodies one last time, a vision that was now burned in his brain. The job was almost done, and now his friends were safe; he'd fixed most of the damage that he'd caused. Except for Cam, and there was no fixing that. Carefully clambering aboard *Dancer*, he said to Rikki, "Time to go."

Rik replied, "Uncleat the bow line."

Rut untied and tossed the line overboard that ran from *Mangoritaville's* stern. The monofilament line which was still attached to her throttles then came tight and pulled them forward to the wide-open-throttle position. As *Mangoritaville* accelerated, the two boats began to separate and the tension on the monofilament increased. It quickly reached its breaking point and snapped, somewhere back near *Dancer's* spring cleat. Rut wound up the loose line then gingerly made his way back to the lean seat with Rikki. She offered him the helm, but he shook his head.

"I want to watch and make sure my ignition pile worked."

Rikki pushed the throttles forward, turning and setting a course for New Inlet. Rut turned to watch as *Mangoritaville* sped off into the night. Rik watched the radar as the blip that was *Mangoritaville* continued moving outward on the screen. It was soon their only reference, as they'd lost sight of her running lights in under two minutes, though Rut continued watching in the now phantom boat's direction.

A few minutes later Rut said, "She's lit."

Rikki glanced back and could see a small orange glow on the horizon. As she watched, it seemed to get brighter. The wind from its movement was undoubtedly forcing more oxygen into the fire, feeding it like a blowtorch. As soon as the cabin windows blow out and the entire superstructure becomes engulfed, the boat should only have a few minutes left. Two minutes later her speed seemed to slow on the radar screen, and they saw a much larger glow that erupted and then finally dimmed.

Rut said, "Gas tanks."

Rikki nodded. Then three minutes after that, the blip disappeared from the radar screen. "She's gone."

"Yep."

"Give me your revolver." When Rut handed it to her, she tossed it overboard.

"Hey! I loved that gun!"

"Just be glad that Mango did too. I'm sure you'll find another one though that you'll love just as much. No loose ends, Rut. You took down two men with your weapons. We don't want any slug matches on the offhand chance that any bodies were to float up out here or at Daniels's. Now the Glock." She held her hand out.

"Not that one, too!"

"Not the whole pistol, just the barrel." Even in the darkness Rik had the slide off and the barrel removed in seconds, then she threw the barrel overboard. "You can get a replacement."

"You're pretty practiced at all of this... but I thought you only had a little company that runs *Bayside*'s security."

"We do that as kind of a sideline, but we're a lot bigger than that; we have people on both coasts. And we solve embarrassing problems for the government in gray areas where they don't like to tread. We provide the plausible deniability that they want and need, and in return, we're well paid for that work. I'm mostly in the office these days because as you saw, I'm a little rusty on the field stuff myself, letting that guy get my weapon away from me like that."

All of this caught Rut off guard. "Looked pretty practiced to me, especially at the lighthouse. And look, I know you didn't do any of this to help me, you did it to help your friends, but... thanks, Rikki." In the dim glow from the data screens, he saw her nod.

"You want to run your boat now?"

"If you don't mind, would you do it for a while? My side is killing me, and I want to rest my eyes for a few minutes."

"Sure, no problem." She watched him climb slowly up onto the lean seat, wedge his feet against the console, his back against the removable backrest, and finally close his eyes. Fortunately, the swells weren't that big, and the distance between them was long. *Dancer* rode over each smoothly, like a kid in a sled on a snow-covered bunny hill. "By the way, Rut, you can still call me Rik."

From behind his closed eyes he said, "I thought you only let your friends call you Rik."

"So, what's your point, Sean?"

He smiled, "Guess I don't have one, Rik."

Despite the trouble that followed him which had put her old friends in jeopardy, Rik couldn't help but like Rut. He'd proven himself today, first by saving Cam and then saving both her and himself by shooting Mango. She knew that even if she hadn't come with him, he would've gone by himself, though that would've been the equivalent of suicide. He'd been determined to protect those that he'd inadvertently put in harm's way, wanting to make things right, even though most of the ones he'd done that for had undoubtedly shut him out now. She thought back about how Rev had tried protecting him by being so careful and selective with his answers to her about Rut. Today she'd gotten a glimpse of why. Dawn had told her that on the phone call Mango said Rut never lied to him, and had always been too honest for his own good. It wasn't meant to be a compliment, at least coming from Mango, but in Rik's book that's exactly how she counted it.

Again she looked over at Rut, who appeared to be asleep now. His chin was resting on his chest, only moving ever so slightly as they crested each swell. She knew the full impact of the day had yet to hit him, and when it did, it was going to be a heavy burden to bear, not that losing Cam wasn't bad enough. You never fully get over taking that first human life. Cam was a good example of that, having had to relive her nightmare from years ago, and teetering on the brink today when she did. She could've gotten up and walked straight out of that room, but the demons from her past demanded she extract that extra pound of flesh, literally. Rik doubted that she'd ever be totally free from what happened back then, and today.

Rik made a mental note to check on Cam later, and to get Rev to check in on Rut. He'd told her he hoped at some point to be able to save Rut's soul, and this may just be the opportunity he'd been waiting for. While Rik wasn't fanatically religious, she was still a believer, and not getting Rev to talk with his old friend right now wasn't an option. It's funny because, in a way, Rut was more free now than he'd been in years. But she suspected the cost for that freedom might have been bigger than even he realized it would be.

Rut hadn't had the chance to really get to know Casey, Dawn, and their friends, all of whom would drop everything and help each other on a minute's notice, just like she had done today. That meant whether it required working inside the law or out, so long as what was needed stayed within their own moral code. Killing these three men today fell outside of that law, but was definitely still inside their unwritten, unspoken code. Rik had a couple of friends outside of this group that she'd be willing to do the same for, and after he killed Mango tonight, Rut was now added to that list. There was no doubt in her mind that Mango planned on shooting them just like he had his own lieutenant, Frankie. The world wouldn't miss him, or any of his crew.

. . .

Two hours later, Rik throttled back as she approached the boatyard's channel. She reached over and gently shook Rut's shoulder. He startled, his eyes popping open.

"Owww, my freaking side feels like it's on fire."

"Getting shot will do that, you know."

"I do now. Hey, I'm sorry, I meant to take the helm for at least part of the ride back."

"You needed your sleep. I wasn't the one who got shot."

"I'm going to take a couple of pain pills that I have stashed away, and hopefully go back to sleep."

She watched him scan the parking area by his house, and saw the crestfallen expression replace the slightly hopeful one when he only saw Daniels's, Rik's, and his own vehicle. He's not one to totally abandon hope, she thought. It was another part of what she was beginning to like about him.

After getting a few hours of sleep, Rik grabbed one of the extra Glock barrels they kept in the armory at her office and drove back over to Rut's boatyard. She walked into his office but didn't find anyone there. As she walked back into the 'yard, a large black man approached her.

"Can I help you, ma'am?"

"I'm looking for Rut."

"He's not workin' today. You wanna leave a message?"

She saw Rut's truck still in the same place it had been last night. "No thanks, I'll catch him over at the house."

Walking over, she knocked at his door but got no answer. She tried the knob and found the door was unlocked.

"Rut?" She started through the door. The bedroom door was open, and she saw him lying on the bed. Again she called out, "Rut?" Again there was no answer, and he didn't move. She rushed over and started shaking him, only to find that he was burning up with fever, and wouldn't wake up. She looked at his wound then hit a speed dial number on her phone. "Doc? I need you over at the house at *Mockhorn Boat Works*, and bring your van. I've got an unconscious male, around forty, with an oozing GS wound. Yeah, he's one of ours."

CASEY WAS in an afternoon meeting with Kari and Cam, who had shown up today like nothing had happened. He was a little nervous about working with her at first, after knowing what she'd done to their captor. It was obvious she had some unresolved issues that probably needed to be worked out. It was the "unknowns" about her that now worried him.

Dawn told him last night that Rik had texted her that "thumbs-up," indicating that things had gone well after she and Rut had left. But now he was surprised by a text from her before they'd had the chance to meet face to face to talk about how things went down.

*"Ran into rough water last night, had some boat damage."*

He texted back, *"Your boat?"*

*"The other one. Didn't think it was that bad at the time, but in the light of day, it's pretty bad."*

*"Where are u?"*

*"House at the boatyard. Know it's not your boat any longer and you might not care because of that, but I figured you ought to know. I'd have sunk without help from that other crew."*

*"On my way."*

He stood up as the others looked at him questioningly. Kari knew it wasn't like Casey to abruptly leave meetings. "You guys carry on, I have to go... somewhere." He involuntarily gave Cam a nervous glance.

"What is it, Casey?" Cam asked.

"I don't know yet. When I find out more from Rik, I'll let you know."

"Is it about Rut?"

He hesitated, then nodded. As she watched him leave, she felt a sudden chill, and was filled with dread.

"Are you all right, Cam?" Kari asked.

"I don't know. I'll tell you after I hear something more from Casey."

As Casey pulled up to Rut's, he saw a white, unmarked panel van backed up by his front door. Once inside the house, he saw Rev sitting with Rik. Both were facing Rut's bedroom door, which was closed. Their faces looked grim.

"How is he? Do we need to take him to the Emergency Room?"

Rik shook her head. "We have our own doc on staff. If we take him to the ER, by law they have to call the police because it's a gunshot wound. At the very least, Rut would go to jail after he recovers. If he recovers. Our doc is working on him now, and we should know more in a bit, but he was burning up and unresponsive when I found him this afternoon. Has to be a bad infection. It was a through and through in his side, but the bullet had already gone through someone else first."

Casey grimaced, then said, "But you said he saved your life?"

"The guy the bullet passed through was Mango's lieutenant, shot by his own boss, and we were next. Rut tricked him, tossing that shiny revolver of his on the deck over to the side, then shot him with his second gun when Mango turned and went for it. Kept shooting him, too. He's not somebody you want pissed at you."

"I thought you weren't a fan of his either," Casey said.

"I didn't like how his past put all of you in danger. But I learned a lot about him yesterday, including how he was going to go with or without me. He knew he'd brought danger to your door, and even though it was unintended, that was weighing heavily on him. He has a big conscience. To him, this was all about making things right, not about saving his own skin."

Rev spoke up, "That's the Rut I've known most of my life, Casey. That's who he is."

The bedroom door opened, and the doctor came out, peeling off gloves and a scrubs tunic. He looked at Rik, "When the bullet passed through the first person it mushroomed, which explains the larger size of his entry wound. But the copper cladding on the bullet peeled back, leaving ragged edges that gathered bacteria and tissue as it passed through the first guy's GI tract. Then it snagged a small piece of the fabric from his shirt that ended up mixed in with the bacteria in the wound canal, leaching out even more of that infectious stew. If you hadn't found him when you did, he'd have been dead in a couple more hours.

"I've flushed out the wound, put in a drain, and closed both the entry and exits. But the biggest problem is that the infection has now spread throughout his body, including up into his brain. I've hit him with a big dose of antibiotics, and now he'll need a continued course through an IV drip. He's going to need someone with him 24/7 until he gets through this. If he gets through this."

Rik said, "That bad?"

"The worst one I've seen. He's lucky you stopped by when you did. If he makes it through tonight and tomorrow, he's got a shot at it. Not much more that could be done for him in a hospital; he'd still get the same drugs, but they'd come along with a pair of metal bracelets. I'll send someone over to stay with him."

Rik said, "I'll be staying with him."

"I will too, Rik," Cam said as she walked in through the door.

Rik looked up at her in surprise, then smiled thinly and nodded. "We'll take shifts."

The doctor looked hesitant at first until he saw the determined look on Rik's face and remembered it was her name on the bottom of his paychecks. "Okay. I'll be back first thing in the morning, and you have me on speed dial if you see any changes. Let me show you both what to look for in his breathing and blood pressure, and if there are any changes, call me immediately. I'll show you how to change the IV solution, since you're going to stay with him. But don't expect him to wake up anytime soon." The van the doc drove was like a portable pharmacy and medical supply, not an ambulance. He had hooked Rut up to monitors identical to those you'd find in the ICU of a hospital. The doc then left plenty of IV bags to replace those on the metal "tree" next to Rut's bed.

After Rev and Casey left, the two women pulled chairs up next to the bed. Cam wanted to know all the details of what happened yesterday through this morning, and Rik gave her the full rundown.

"So, he was still going to go over to Mango's boat even if you weren't?" Cam asked.

"You saw how he wanted to set right the wrongs that he'd been responsible for bringing into everyone else's lives. He wasn't going to leave it unfinished."

"Whether you were with him or not. That would have been nuts to go alone. Stupid and insane." Cam shook her head sadly.

Rik nodded. "Honestly, I don't know if he expected to come back. His attitude changed after you walked away on the dock. That's what made him more determined to finish it by going after Mango. By the way, why did you come back? He was convinced you two were done. Heck, I was too."

Cam looked down, took his hand in hers and said, "Because I realized I've been falling in love with him, even after he made me so angry. I haven't straight up told him that, I'd only hinted at it." She looked over at his now pale face, "Do you hear me, Sean Rutledge? You've gotta fight and get through this because I'm not going anywhere after you do."

# 21

# COINCIDENCES

Late that afternoon Dawn breezed into the salon of *Lady Dawn* and made a beeline for the bar in the far corner. Casey was sitting on one of the couches, and with her back to him, she poured a vodka on the rocks while giving him a slight rundown on her first day of grand jury duty.

"The grand jury duty is really not as bad as I thought it would be, except for this young attorney. And believe it or not, I *was* elected the foreman. I can't tell you much more than that, but things went very well." She turned around with her drink, and that's when she noticed how somber he looked. "Casey, what's wrong?"

Casey gave her the full version of events. Dawn sat down next to him, staring off into space, almost forgetting her cocktail. She said, "I was so angry with him, thinking he was only out for himself at anyone else's expense."

"We all were. But he didn't think Mango would be after you. He had no way of knowing that Mango's case would be going in front of the grand jury. And according to Rev, he'd gone through hell with a divorce and then almost losing his business. Borrowing from Mango had been a last-ditch effort to keep from losing everything that was left. And once he was under that guy's thumb, it was next to impossible for him to get away. Ironically, he moved Cam into his place so he could help protect her, but that was where that Joey guy first saw her. After I heard the whole story from Rik and Rev, I realized he really was the guy we'd originally believed him to be. He made a stupid mistake, actually, a couple of them. Unfortunately, we ended up getting caught in the wake of those. Heck, I've made mistakes that cost other people as well as me, so I'm not all that different, Dawn."

"Oh, you're a lot different, Casey. But this does put a different light on things."

"We were so quick to forget about him jumping in to save you."

"After my husband and my new friend got kidnapped because of something he did, yeah I think we can get a pass on that."

"He was trying to fix what he'd done wrong, and I kind of feel like I want to do the same for him. Let's grab some food from the *Cafe* and take it up there for Rik and Cam and whoever else might be sitting with him."

~

HE FELT SO HOT, *he thought. And now there were voices that drifted in and out with the pain that wracked his entire body. He was sure he was imagining them. Some sounded like Dawn, Casey, and Cam, but they were all gone from his life, so he knew he must be hallucinating. As he began to drift back into the abyss where the pain couldn't reach him, he felt someone squeeze his hand right before he fell off the cliff and away from the pain. In that brief second before the fall, he squeezed back.*

"RUT! Rut! If you can hear me, squeeze my hand again," Cam said. She turned to the others, who had now stopped talking and were focused on her. "I squeezed his hand, and for a second he squeezed mine back! C'mon Rut, please squeeze my hand again." She stared intently at his hand, but wasn't rewarded with another squeeze. His face stayed pale and slack.

"This came on so fast," Rikki said. "He was in pain when we got back, but not more than I've seen before with people who've been shot. He was going to take some pain pills then get some rest. Damn it, I should've called the doc last night."

"Don't beat yourself up, Rik. You saved him once yesterday as it is," Dawn said.

"And he has saved every one of us in this room except Rev. I hate not being able to take him to the hospital, but I'd hate what that would mean afterward even more. So long as he gets the same care here..."

Someone knocked at the door, catching all of them off guard. But the knocking itself wasn't nearly as surprising as the identity of who did it. Dawn answered the door and was stunned to find Assistant US Attorney Ron Devaro, with FBI Special Agent Stephanie Baker standing behind him on the porch. Dawn had spent the day with Devaro, since he was the one spearheading the indictment of Mango. Baker was not just an FBI agent, but a friend who had once saved Casey's life. But the young, overly aggressive, and cocky lawyer Devaro didn't have many fans on the grand jury, including Dawn.

"What the hell are you doing here?" Devaro demanded.

"Tending to a friend who's hurt. Hello, Stephanie."

"Hello, Dawn. We're here to interview Sean Rutledge, but how do you know Devaro?"

He interrupted, "She's on my grand jury, that's how. And right now, she's standing in the home of someone who may have information on a case that she's already heard, which now makes it a potential minefield. The more obvious question is how do you know her, Baker?"

"Her husband Casey was with me when I shot 'Jimmy the Eye' Impasato, who had been after him. We've all been friends ever since," Baker said.

"Oh, great. It would have been nice to have known all of this earlier today, Mrs. Shaw. The mob was after your husband?"

"I'd have been happy to tell you, Mr. Devaro, if you'd have asked me any questions along those lines during voir dire. But yes, a renegade member of the mob had been out to get him a while back. Casey wounded him and Stephanie finished him off, and after that, it was no longer an issue."

Baker quickly said, "Mr. Shaw was cleared of any wrongdoing, Devaro. Dawn, we need to see a Mr. Sean Rutledge, can we come in?"

"Of course, Stephanie, but unfortunately it won't do you any good, Rut has had an accident, is very ill, and currently unconscious. Come on in though, I think you know most everyone here."

"Tonight just keeps getting better and better since my lead investigator is a friend of everyone in a potential witness's home. Where's Rutledge?" Devaro was using his most sarcastic tone.

Dawn pointed at the bedroom door. "In there. Another friend is sitting with him."

While Devaro went into the bedroom, Stephanie asked, "I don't suppose you want to tell me how you know Sean Rutledge, Dawn?"

Dawn gave her a quick and abbreviated version of the attack on her at the marina, and their subsequent friendship. Then Devaro came back into the room.

"Why isn't this man in a hospital?"

Thinking fast Rikki answered, "He doesn't have any health insurance, and before he became unconscious, he said he wanted to stay at home. Luckily, I have a friend who is a private physician, and he's treating him here as a favor to me. Rut's a friend of mine, and does a lot for people around the waterfront."

Devaro seemed to weigh this information then asked, "What happened to him?"

"He slipped and fell on a grapple hook anchor that was on the deck of his boat. One of the prongs went right through his side. He treated it himself, but since it happened on a fishing boat it became infected, then went into sepsis," Rikki said as Devaro winced at the mental image.

"Do any of you know if he borrowed money from a loan shark named Michael "Mango" Magnowski?"

Rikki chuckled, "Look around this room. If Rut needed to borrow money, he could raise whatever he needs from one or all of us, or we'd help him get commercial financing. He wouldn't need to borrow a cent from any loan shark."

"He was seen with Magnowski at *Mallard Cove*."

"Rut talks to everybody at *Mallard Cove*, he's a regular there. Does this guy you're talking about have a boat?" Rikki asked. When Devaro nodded, she said, "Rut's boatyard is one of the least expensive in Virginia. Maybe this guy Margo was shopping prices."

"He goes by Mango, not Margo. Well, that's possible, I guess. But this room is certainly filled with coincidences, which is not something I like. And both Magnowski and his boat disappeared today, just before he was about to be arrested."

Casey finally spoke up. "I don't really care what you do or don't like. Rut saved my wife from drowning, and you can call that a coincidence if you want, but Reverend Jones here," he pointed at Rev, "and I call it a miracle. And we're all now praying for another one. You're welcome to join us in that, or you can feel free to get the hell out of here. You can see that Rut is in no shape to answer any questions, and might not ever be again."

Devaro turned to Dawn, totally ignoring Casey. "You knew about Magnowski's indictment, since you are the foreman on the grand jury."

"Are you accusing me of something? Because if you are, you had better get your facts straight or you'll be prosecuting parking tickets! Just when did Magnowski and his boat disappear?" Dawn demanded.

"Sometime prior to 3 p.m., when the indictment came down."

"So, you mean during the time I was with you. In a federal courthouse where I had no access to any communication device, and was in the company of two dozen other people, including a court reporter. Yeah, hot shot, you got me. I was in contact with him through mental telepathy, this man I've never met. You know, your abundant arrogance doesn't make up for your sad lack of intelligence. If you had any brains, you'd see we're all here worried about Rut, and you aren't wanted here."

Devaro bristled, "And you need to be at the Federal Courthouse half an hour early tomorrow. You and I are going to have a talk with the judge, because I want you off my jury."

"Yeah, well, that makes two of us."

Devaro turned on his heel and walked out the front door.

Stephanie glanced sideways at both Casey and Dawn then shook her head slightly before walking out, a small smile on her face. She was obviously not a Devaro fan, and apparently happy to have seen Casey and Dawn both tell him off.

After watching them drive away, Dawn grinned widely and said, "Well, it looks like I owe Rut another favor. Getting me off jury duty is huge."

"Yeah, so long as you aren't in huge trouble for not being forthcoming," Rik said.

"Hey, he never asked if I knew Rut, Mango, or Stephanie. Never asked if I had a relative the mob wanted to kill, either. So, screw him. That guy has a really huge unearned opinion of himself, and I have the blanket immunity thing that automatically comes with being on a grand jury. So long as he sticks to how I met Rut tomorrow, I should be good. I don't think he'll want to dwell too much on how he missed all that stuff during voir dire this morning by not asking enough questions."

∽

THREE DAYS LATER...

"AND AS SOON AS you're able, we need to go back offshore and get more fresh mahi. I never did make you that Mahi à la Française. Heck, I haven't made you much of anything yet. You don't even know if you like how I cook, though I know I like how you grill. I do make a mean Oysters Rockefeller, by the way. I hope you like shellfish. And clams, I love clams. There have to be some good clam bars around here where we can go dig our own. Linguini with clam sauce is another specialty of mine." Cam looked at Rut's face, seeing there'd been no change in the last three days. "Rut, please come back. The doctor says your bloodwork is getting better, and that you may be able to hear me even though your eyes aren't open yet. So I'm going to talk your ear off until they are."

"Hey, Cam!" Rikki called out as she came in the front door.

"In here talking to Rut."

Rik walked into the room, "He say anything yet or open his eyes?"

Cam shook her head. "Nothing. But I'm going to keep trying, and I'm not leaving his side until he's up and out of bed." She paused a minute then said quietly, "I should have been there with you guys, Rik."

"This wasn't your fault, Cam. You need to quit beating yourself up over it. He was right in telling you that you weren't coming with us. And remember, I said the same thing to you. These things happen when thugs like Mango are involved. Even the best plan can go sideways, like that one did."

"Hey! Rik, he just squeezed my hand again! Rut, can you hear me? He did it again!"

"I'll call the doc."

LATER THAT DAY in the kitchen the doctor briefed Rik and Cam. "He's making a lot of progress, and as soon as he's able we'll try getting him up and out of bed. But that infection has taken quite a toll on his system, so it'll be a few weeks before he's back to a hundred percent. Fortunately, his bloodwork shows there was no liver damage, and he's definitely on the mend. So, make him take things slowly, one step at a time. But I do expect him to make a full recovery."

From the bedroom came a hoarse voice, "Can... I... have... a... soda?" Cam jumped up from the table and raced in.

The doctor smiled at Rikki. "And that's a big step."

# EPILOGUE

F*ifteen days later...*

Rut was resting in a chair on his porch when Cam brought his mail over from the boatyard office. "Big Jim said he had to sign for this one, so it must be important."

She handed him the stack, with the certified envelope on top. The return address was a law firm in Melfa. He tore open the envelope, and read the single page it contained. Then he dialed the number on the letterhead, put the phone on speaker, and asked to speak to the attorney who had signed the letter. After a minute Randall Jameson came on the phone.

"Mr. Rutledge, thank you for your call. We might want to schedule an appointment in my office..."

Rut interrupted, "I had an accident, and I'm not yet back at work, Randall."

"Oh, I see. Well, your address isn't that far from my office, I guess I could come there if you are up to having a chat. Are you available this afternoon, say around four?"

"Not planning on going anywhere."

"Then I'll see you at four."

After he hung up, Cam looked at him curiously. Rut said, "Something about the estate of Hubert Daniels, and this guy Jameson is the executor. Funny, I never knew Daniels's first name before this. Probably wants to take custody of the car."

"I guess you'll know for sure at four."

"Yeah. I guess I could've driven over there. I mean, I feel fine, but I don't like being beckoned, especially by lawyers."

"THANK YOU FOR SEEING ME, Mr. Rutledge."

"Thanks for making the house call, Randall. And call me Rut, if you don't mind. So, I'm assuming you want to take custody of Daniels's car. It's right over there, and the keys are in it. He always left the keys here in case we ever had to move it."

"Uh, Rut, I'm sorry but I wanted to talk about this in person instead of over the phone. The car, his boat, as well as all his personal property were left in a foundation that is to benefit other watermen in Virginia, and especially on ESVA. The state of course took title to his home, such as it is."

"I'm confused here, Randall, what has this got to do with me?"

"Mr. Daniels named you as the president of this organization, and said that you would know which watermen were in true need of a hand up, not a handout. He left this letter for you."

*"HEY RUT, you've been good to me and so many other water working folk, and I'd like your help keeping that going. If you don't mind, I'd like you to head this trust thing up that Jameson put together. Pick some good folk that are in need of a hand up, like you've already been doing. You got to give away ten percent of the total every year to keep it from being taxed, but then you keep investing the rest, which should keep it going a good while. Oh, and you get to keep ten percent of everything you give away for your trouble. And don't sell the car, there's a lot of water folk that could use one*

that runs that good. And my skiff and gear, too. Find some kid who wants to own a live bait business an' help him or her get started. The state's gonna to grab my place, but the kid could find some other place to run it from.

"Anyhoo, thanks for being a pal all these years, and I hope you'll do this thing for me. Probably be a pain in the ass with all the paperwork, which is why you get to keep some of it. I promise that it'll be the last favor I ask you. And I'll be waiting on you when it's your turn to 'cross the bar.'

"Daniels"

Rut looked up, "Lots of paperwork?"

"A fair bit, but my office can advise you on it. You need to know that this is easily a lifetime of work. Properly reinvested, it could be a self-perpetuating foundation, even with the annual dispersals and expenses. Of course, you aren't limited to disbursing only ten percent annually, but his intent was to help people, not make them rich."

"Rich? Just how much is in this thing?"

"Outside of the boat and the car, a little under ten million, mostly in stocks and bonds. Hubert was a pretty astute investor."

Rut laughed at the joke, then noticed that Randall wasn't smiling. "You're serious? You mean... dollars?" He asked incredulously after a pause.

"It's not pesos."

"I knew Daniels had to have some money, but *damn!* I never thought it was that much. He was always so tight with a buck."

Randall nodded. "He left everything to that foundation and lived mostly off the money that he made from catching bait. This was something he wanted to do, leave a legacy that he and his family would be remembered for among those that work these waters. He wanted to repay you through it for everything that you've done over the years for both him and the rest of the working waterfront community. So, is this something that you are willing to do?"

"Absolutely."

"Okay, the first thing is, I received a call from the Lynnhaven Police. Apparently, Hubert's boat somehow ended up at a marina down there, and my office address is on the registration. Do you have people that can go bring it back? I'm assuming you'll want to dock it here until you find the right candidate for it."

"Yes. We'll clean it up, and make sure it's in perfect running condition. I'll do the work myself, so it won't cost anything."

Randall smiled. "I think Hubert made a very wise choice when he picked you."

AFTER JAMESON LEFT, Cam came out of the house, having wanted to give Rut privacy with the attorney. She sat on the front edge of the chair next to his. When he told her the full story, she was just as stunned as he had been. "So what are you going to do?" She asked.

"I'm going to do it, and I'm going to hire Rev as a consultant. He knows everybody on the waterfront, as well as their needs. He'll know the good candidates, as well as the ones who will only want a handout so they can sit on their butts. There are plenty of both around ESVA, and I want to find the right ones."

"What about the boatyard?"

"This foundation thing isn't a full-time job, but I figure on giving Big Jim more responsibility as well as a raise. I'll get him to take up the slack for me. Plus, that'll give me more time to renovate boats, doing what I like most of all. What about you?"

Cam looked confused, "What?"

"It's been almost three weeks, and you haven't been back to the Shaws'. Are you going back to work for them or not?"

"It was kind of hard to take care of you and work down there at the same time."

Rut said, "You're avoiding my question."

"And they started avoiding you once you were awake again."

"They don't owe me anything. They're busy people, and we're barely acquaintances. I never counted on them hanging around the boatyard. But you're still avoiding my question."

Cam sighed and sat all the way back in her chair. "I think Casey feels uncomfortable around me now, you know, after I cut Joey's 'junk' off him. I think that's a big part of why we haven't heard from them."

Rut laughed for the first time since he recovered.

"I'm serious, Rut. It's like I make him nervous."

"Cam, it's a guy thing. Most of us feel guilty as hell taking a dog in to be neutered. Have you ever driven down I-95 in Florida? There's a doctor that advertises vasectomies on several billboards with his big smiling face on them, saying he's done more of these procedures than anyone else. It gives me the creeps every time I see one of those things. If I walked into a bar and saw him sitting there, I'd find another place to drink."

"Rut, that's not funny. I'm serious."

"And I was too, at least partly. Look, I think if you give it some time, things will settle out."

"It's never going to be the same, my relationship with Dawn and him. I think I'll get another server job at a different restaurant, and pay them back their signing bonus as I can."

Rut was quiet for a moment then said, "I'll pay them back for you. It's the least I can do since this is all my fault and you took such good care of me, I owe you big time. And why don't you come in with me on renovating boats? We can split the work and the profits, I mean if you want to. You seemed to have a natural knack for pushing sandpaper," he grinned.

She said, "Can I have overnight to think about that?"

"Take as long as you'd like. Hey, you know what? I feel like taking my first post-recovery boat ride. We're going up to the *Bluffs* for dinner again, but this time I'm running *Dancer*."

~

4:30 A.M. *the next day...*

RUT SAT bolt upright on hearing someone pounding on their front door. He grabbed the Glock and went to the door with Cam right behind him. Instead of opening the door he shouted, "Who the hell's there?"

"Friends bringing beer, bait, and tackle," Sandy Morgan replied.

Rut turned on the porch light and swung open the door. Sandy stood there along with Casey and Dawn. Beyond them he saw a massive sportfisherman tied up at the dock, its cockpit awash in floodlights and its running lights on. "What are you all doing here?"

Dawn said, "We brought *Sharke* up from North Carolina yesterday, and heard that you had gone to dinner at the *Bluffs* by boat last night. One of the benefits of owning the place is we hear about these kinds of things. Anyway, we figured if you could make that run, then you should be up for *Sharke's* inaugural fishing trip this morning. Sandy was dying to pay you back for his early morning wakeup anyway, so here we are. So, c'mon, let's go! Eric, Missy, and Rik are already aboard, and we have breakfast ready."

Casey added, "And speaking of being ready, now that Rut's back on his feet as well as the water, I'm hoping you're ready to come back to work on Monday, Cam. Kari has a ton of work lined up for you. Sorry we haven't been in touch in a while, we've been down in Carolina doing all the sea trials and shakedown stuff on *Sharke*. But we'll have plenty of time to talk about all that out on the water. There are mahi out there with our names on them, so grab your gear and some fishing clothes and let's go!"

∼

THERE'S STILL MORE in store for the gang from Mallard Cove. The next book in the series, Coastal Currency, is already waiting for you at Amazon.com. Get your copy now!

*Coastal Jury*

# GLOSSARY

I grew up on the water in South Florida, and I have an extensive boating background. I've worked on boats, built them, re-built them, and spent a good amount of time in boatyards. I've always loved boats, and ever since I was a pre-teenager, I haven't gone longer than six months without owning at least one. Most of my friends are boaters, too. So it's easy for me to forget that not everyone is as familiar with the jargon as my friends and me, which is something that I've now been reminded of on more than one occasion. (My apologies to those readers that I ended up sending to the dictionary!) To make amends, here's a (growing) list of uniquely nautical terms and words that have been included in several of my books. Bear in mind that these definitions are based on my own usage and experience. Things can be different from one region to another. For instance, you can fish for stripers in Montauk, New York, but here in Virginia, we fish for rockfish. But the true name for the target species is "striped bass."

So, here are the definitions of some of the more confusing words, at least as I know them. We'll start with a half dozen simple ones, then move on to those that are more complex:

*Coastal Jury*

- **Bow:** the front of the boat.
- **Stern:** back of the boat.
- **Port:** the left side of the boat.
- **Starboard:** the right side of the boat.
- **Aft:** the rear of the boat.
- **Forward:** (fore) the front of the boat.
- **Bow Thruster:** a propeller in a tube that is mounted from side to side through the bow below the waterline, allowing the captain more maneuverability and control when docking especially in adverse winds and current. Powered by an electric or hydraulic motor.
- **Bulkhead:** boat wall.
- **Center Console:** a type of boat with a raised helm console in the middle of the boat with space on each side to walk around. Most also incorporate a built-in bench seat or cooler seat in the front.
- **Chine:** the longitudinal area running fore and aft where the bottom meets the side. It can be rounded or "sharp." They hurt when the boat rocks and it meets your head when you are swimming next to it. Trust me on that.
- **Circle Hook:** a fishhook designed to get caught in the corner of a fish's mouth. Greatly reduces the mortality of fish that are released or that break the line.
- **Citation:** at an airport, it's a type of jet made by Cessna. But here in Virginia, it's a slip of paper suitable for framing, issued by the state confirming that you caught a fish that's considered large for its particular species. Or it can be a speeding ticket, either on water or land. I like the fish kind better.
- **Covering Board:** a flat surface at the top of a gunwale usually made out of teak or fiberglass, that's used as a step for boarding and for mounting recessed rod holders.
- **Deck:** what floors on boats are called.

- **Fighting Chair:** a specialized chair that can be turned to face a fish. Mounted on a sturdy stanchion with a built-in gimbal, the chair allows the angler to use the attached footrest to use their legs and body to gain more leverage on a large fish. Most of today's fighting chairs are based on the design by my late friend John Rybovich.
- **Fish Box:** a built-in storage box for the day's catch. They can be either elevated in the stern, or in the deck with a flush-mounted lid. Some of the higher-end sportfish boats have cooling systems or automatic ice makers that continually add ice throughout the trip.
- **Fishing Cockpit:** the lower aft deck on a sportfisherman that usually contains a fighting chair, fish box, baitwell, and tackle center. Surrounded on three sides by the gunwales and the stern. The cockpit deck is usually just above the waterline, with scuppers that drain overboard. Can get flooded when backing down hard on a big fish.
- **Flying Bridge (Flybridge):** a permanently mounted helm area on top of the wheelhouse. Can be open or enclosed.
- **Following Sea:** when the waves are moving toward the boat from behind the stern.
- **Gaff:** a large, usually barbless hook at the end of a pole, used for landing fish. They come in different sizes and lengths.
- **Gangway (Gangplank):** a removable ramp or set of stairs attached to the side of larger boats to allow easier access for boarding from a dock. Usually hinged to allow for tide variation.
- **Gear:** marine transmission which has forward, neutral, and reverse.
- **Gimbal:** there are a few types, but the ones in my books are rod holders with swivels built into fighting chairs.
- **Gin Pole:** a vertical pole next to the gunwale usually rigged with a block and tackle and used for hauling large

fish aboard. These used to be quite common until John Rybovich invented the transom door fifty years ago.
- **Gunwale (pronounced gun-nul):** aft side area of a boat above the waterline, also the area on either side of a fishing cockpit.
- **Hatch:** a hole in a deck or bulkhead with a cover that may be hinged or completely removable. On a sportfisherman, the door into the wheelhouse may be called either a hatch or a door.
- **Head:** a bathroom, or a marine toilet.
- **Helm:** the area that includes the steering and engine controls. In many sportfishing boats, the controls are mounted on a helm pod, a wood box with radiused edges that juts out of a cabinet or bulkhead.
- **Keys Conch:** a person born in the Florida Keys. You can be born in Miami and move to the Keys an hour later, then live down there the rest of your life, and you will still NEVER be a Conch. They are usually very tough and independent characters.
- **Lean Seat:** a high bench seat usually found behind the helm of a center console. Designed to be leaned against or sat upon. May have storage built-in under the seat section.
- **Mezzanine Deck:** a shallow, raised deck on a sportfish just forward of the fishing cockpit, and aft of the wheelhouse bulkhead. Usually contains aft facing bench seating for anglers to comfortably watch the baits that are being trolled behind the boat.
- **Outriggers:** long aluminum poles on sportfishing boats that are raked up and aft from up alongside the wheelhouse. They are extended outward when fishing, having clips on lines that carry the fishing lines out away from the boat, creating a wider spread.
- **Pilot Boat:** a smaller boat designed to handle all kinds of seas, whose sole purpose is delivering and retrieving a

- captain with extensive local knowledge to larger boats approaching or leaving a port.
- **Rod Holder:** like the name suggests, a device that a fishing rod butt is inserted into in order to hold it steady. There are recessed types that are mounted in covering boards, and exposed ones attached to railings or tower legs.
- **Salon:** a living room area of a boat's cabin.
- **Scuppers:** deck or cockpit drains.
- **SeaKeeper Gyro:** a stabilizing gyro that almost eliminates roll in boats.
- **Shaft:** attaches a propeller to the gear.
- **Sheer Line:** the rail edge where the foredeck meets the side of the hull.
- **Sonar/Fish Finder:** electronic underwater 'radar' that displays the sea floor, and anything between it and the boat.
- **Sportfisherman (Sportfish):** a unique style of boat designed specifically for fishing.
- **Spread:** the arrangement of the baits being towed while trolling.
- **Stem:** the forwardmost edge of the bow.
- **Stern:** the farthest aft part of the boat, also called the transom.
- **Tackle Center:** a cabinet in the fishing cockpit or the center console which holds hooks, swivels, leads and other fishing supplies.
- **(Tuna) Tower:** an aluminum pipe structure located above the house or the flybridge designed to hold spotters or riders, and may or may not have an additional helm.
- **Transom:** stern.
- **Transom (Tuna) Door:** a door in the stern just above the waterline, designed for boating large fish, but also useful for retrieving swimmers and divers.
- **Trough:** the lowest point between waves.

- **Wheel (Propeller):** slang for a prop.
- **Wheel (Steering):** controls the boat direction.
- **Wheelhouse (House):** the cabin section of a boat which sometimes contains an enclosed helm.

# ABOUT THE AUTHOR

Don Rich is the author of the bestselling Coastal Adventure Series. Three of his books even simultaneously held the top three spots in Amazon's Hot New Releases in Boating.

Don's books are set mainly in the mid-Atlantic because of his love for this stretch of coastline. A fifth generation Florida native who grew up on the water, he has spent a good portion of his life on, in, under, or beside it.

He now makes his home in central Virginia. When he's not writing or watching another fantastic mid-Atlantic sunset, he can often be found on the Chesapeake or the Atlantic with a fishing rod in his hand.

Don loves to hear from readers, and you can reach him via email at contact@donrichbooks.com

# ALSO BY DON RICH

*(Check my website www.DonRichBooks.com or visit Amazon.com)*

### The Coastal Beginnings Series:

*(The prelude to the Coastal Adventure Series)*

- COASTAL CHANGES
- COASTAL TREASURE
- COASTAL RULES
- COASTAL BLUFFS

### The Coastal Adventure Series:

- COASTAL CONSPIRACY
- COASTAL COUSINS
- COASTAL PAYBACKS
- COASTAL TUNA
- COASTAL CATS
- COASTAL CAPER
- COASTAL CULPRIT
- COASTAL CURSE
- COASTAL JURY
- COASTAL CURRENCY
- COASTAL CRUISE

### Other Books by Don Rich:

- GhostWRITER

Here's A Tropical Authors Novella by Deborah Brown, Nicholas Harvey, and Don Rich:

- **Priceless**

Go to my website at www.DonRichBooks.com for more information about joining my **Reader's Group**! And you can follow me on Facebook at: https://www.facebook.com/DonRichBooks

I'm also a member of TropicalAuthors.com, where you can find my latest books and those by dozens of my coastal writer friends!

TROPICALAUTHORS.COM

Made in the USA
Columbia, SC
17 June 2025